THE STUDENT

H. M. LYNN

First published in Great Britain in 2025 by Boldwood Books Ltd.

Copyright © H. M. Lynn, 2025

Cover Design by Head Design Ltd.

Cover Images: iStock

The moral right of H. M. Lynn to be identified as the author of this work has been asserted in accordance with the Copyright, Designs and Patents Act 1988.

All rights reserved. No part of this book may be reproduced in any form or by any electronic or mechanical means, including information storage and retrieval systems, without written permission from the author, except for the use of brief quotations in a book review. This book is a work of fiction and, except in the case of historical fact, any resemblance to actual persons, living or dead, is purely coincidental.

Every effort has been made to obtain the necessary permissions with reference to copyright material, both illustrative and quoted. We apologise for any omissions in this respect and will be pleased to make the appropriate acknowledgements in any future edition.

A CIP catalogue record for this book is available from the British Library.

Paperback ISBN 978-1-83603-802-3

Large Print ISBN 978-1-83603-801-6

Hardback ISBN 978-1-83603-800-9

Ebook ISBN 978-1-83603-803-0

Kindle ISBN 978-1-83603-804-7

Audio CD ISBN 978-1-83603-795-8

MP3 CD ISBN 978-1-83603-796-5

Digital audio download ISBN 978-1-83603-799-6

This book is printed on certified sustainable paper. Boldwood Books is dedicated to putting sustainability at the heart of our business. For more information please visit https://www.boldwoodbooks.com/about-us/sustainability/

Boldwood Books Ltd, 23 Bowerdean Street, London, SW6 3TN

www.boldwoodbooks.com

ALSO BY H. M. LYNN

The Head Teacher
The Student

H. M. Lynn writing as Hannah Lynn

The Holly Berry Sweet Shop Series
The Sweet Shop of Second Chances
Love Blooms at the Second Chances Sweet Shop
High Hopes at the Second Chances Sweet Shop
Family Ties at the Second Chances Sweet Shop
Sunny Days at the Second Chances Sweet Shop
A Summer Wedding at the Second Chances Sweet Shop

The Wildflower Lock Series
New Beginnings at Wildflower Lock
Coffee and Cake at Wildflower Lock
Blue Skies Over Wildflower Lock

To Sally Wood and all the other foster carers doing an amazing job.

1

I've been sitting in the small room by the university library for ten minutes, and already Duncan's sent me four texts.

> Good luck.
>
> Don't get stressed and flustered, you can do this.
>
> Not to put too much pressure on you, but we could really do with this money.
>
> But it doesn't matter if you don't get it. Love you.

Considering I never normally get more than two texts a day full stop, it's clear he's as nervous about this interview as I am, and his nerves aren't helping me.

I turn my phone over on the table and draw in a long breath. I shouldn't blame him. It is a big deal. Interview anxiety kept me up all of last night and made it impossible for me to think about anything else all day. This interview, this meeting, isn't just about the money. It could be the start of everything for me. Everything I've ever wanted. Not to mention it would be confirmation that I was right to take a risk and start a degree when so much of me believed the opportunity was past.

In most adult circumstances, five years isn't much of an age gap. Plenty of people find happy relationships with a far greater difference in age, and friendships, well, they can span decades, right? But when you start university, and you're five years older than your peers, it shows. I didn't come here as a bright-eyed eighteen-year-old full of hope and optimism. I started as a twenty-four-year-old with a past. A past I didn't want anybody to know about.

My aim was simple: stay off the radar and ensure the only time I was noticed was for my writing. The only time I wanted to draw attention to myself was when a lecturer saw the potential in me to make it in the literary world, and now it's finally happened. Now I'm finally about to get my break.

It was a short story I wrote about two siblings abandoned for several months in a remote costal town that caught Professor Jarvis's attention. He saw potential, he told me. Raw talent that could be harnessed. And he wanted to offer me an opportunity. This opportunity: to interview as a ghost-writer.

'Explain to me what ghost-writers do,' Duncan had said when I came home, bouncing with excitement. I don't think he's ever seen me bounce before. I certainly hadn't been the bouncing type of person when he met me, but I could already feel the difference. This could change everything.

'You write the book,' I told him, 'but someone else's name goes on it.'

'That doesn't seem fair,' he said, and I realised I needed to give more of an explanation than that.

'Sometimes, the clients have the ideas already. They're not writers, so they give you the plot and the concept, and you need to get the words down on paper. Sometimes, you have to guide them a little bit more. Make sure it all makes sense. World-building. Characters. That type of thing.'

'And what's this one you're interviewing for?' he asked.

'I'm not exactly sure,' I admitted. 'All I know about this person is that they go by the name of Dr B. My professor said he'd interviewed several people already for the position, but the client hadn't been happy with any of them. Then Professor Jarvis read my story and thought I might be a good fit.'

Just thinking of the way the professor spoke to me after his lecture last week still causes my chest to burn with pride. I'd honestly forgotten I could feel that way. For someone who's spent their adult life dealing with shame, the sensation was almost unrecognisable. Not for Duncan, though. He's always proud of me.

'You've got this,' Duncan said. 'You're going to be amazing.'

'I don't want to get my hopes up. Like the professor said, other people have interviewed for this position. Other writers who are far more experienced than me.'

'Have a bit of faith in yourself. After everything you've been through, you deserve this break.'

That was the one thing he'd said that I couldn't disagree with. Still, I've been trying not to get ahead of myself, but it's hard. It's really hard. Especially now, when everything is so close, it's almost like I can touch it.

My laptop is still closed in front of me as I drum my fingers against the table, trying to keep myself grounded. Yet my mind flickers to the possible paycheque this job could give me. Duncan and I have been living in a nightmare shared accommodation for the last year. One room with all our belongings, including his guitars and double bass, which leaves little room for anything else. If I get this job, it would mean we would have enough money to rent a place by ourselves.

With a sudden realisation that I haven't yet signed the forms agreeing to the interview, I open up my laptop and find the documents I need to complete, which includes an NDA that prohibits me from talking about the client or sharing my writing, and the bank details where they should send the money, on the slim chance I get the job. Professor Jarvis also told me I had to have everything signed, or the interview wouldn't be able to go ahead. It's a sign of how nervous I am that I almost forgot that. Still, it's a two-minute job before they're all sent off. Then I'm back to waiting.

There's a clock on the wall in front of me, and it says eight forty-five, the same as my watch, the same as the laptop screen. I've still got fifteen more minutes to wait and I know each of them will drag. With a need to pass the time, I open up another document. It's a list of facts about myself – my résumé, I guess, though there's probably not enough on it to call it that. Still, I know I need to have something for when the client asks me what my experience is, and I'm about to read through it as a quick refresher when my phone pings. I assume it's going to be Duncan again, but instead, it's Heidi's name on the screen.

> I hope this evening goes well.

As I stare at the screen, my heart kicks up another notch. I could swear I didn't tell her about the interview. It's not that I don't trust Heidi. I do; she's the only person on the course who knows about my past, but this is the type of thing that would make Heidi jealous. Professor Jarvis told me this isn't something he normally puts students forward for, and it was only because I'm notably older than even some of his PhD students that he felt confident I could manage the situation professionally.

Heidi has enough of an issue with comparing herself to

everyone else as it is. But if it's not for the interview, then what is she talking about? What is she wishing me luck for? I think back through our conversations from earlier today. Mainly we were talking about work that was due in, though I also mentioned how Duncan has a gig tonight. A pretty big one. So that's probably what she's referring to. I ping back a smiley face. I am not an emoji person. I probably like them even less than I like socialising, but I don't have the focus to say more.

When I glance back at the clock, I'm surprised by how quickly the time has passed. It's now only three minutes until this interview starts. My nerves rocket to a place where my pulse is audible against my eardrums and when I look at my laptop, an email has come through. There is no title, no text at all, just a link to a meeting room. With my heart hammering in my chest and a feeling close to nausea sweeping through me, I take a deep breath and click open.

2

There's no waiting. The room is open and apparently both of us are in it, only I struggle to understand what I'm looking at. For a moment, I think the screen is still blank and that they haven't turned the camera on, but there are shadows moving across my image. Organic and varied in a way that wouldn't happen if there was no camera on. After a second, I realise that there is a curtain between the person and me, like this is a police interview and the witness's identity is being concealed.

'Francesca, Francesca, so pleased to meet you. Thank you for agreeing to meet me.'

I try to swallow the lump in my throat, but it's hard to shift. The words aren't spoken by a person. Or at least, not directly. They're synthesised. Not quite monotone, but no inflections. No warmth. The hair on the back of my neck prickles, but I fight the sensation down as I force myself to smile and respond.

'Thank you ever so much for wanting to see me,' I say. 'Before we start, I just want you to know that this is my first interview for a ghost-writing position. I know that you've spoken to several more experienced writers, but obviously, if you think that we're a good fit, I will do the very best job that I am capable of. And while I may not have experience in this nature of writing, I have written for various online and paper outlets. I've had short stories published in several magazines as well. I'm happy to send those to you if you would like to read through them?'

'Well, I have to say, I normally start these interviews by being able to get a word in edgeways.'

A red heat burns my cheeks. Talking through uncomfortable situations has become my default. Probably because I know that if I keep talking and filling the air with words, it will stop other people from saying things I don't want to hear.

'Sorry,' I say. 'Like I said, I'm new to this.'

'I can tell, yes, but I won't hold that against you. We all have to start somewhere. Besides, creativity knows no age limits, don't you agree?'

'Absolutely,' I say, sensing that's the right answer. I don't mention what I actually think about creativity requiring control and discipline to make that happen.

'I need someone who will write a very unique piece of literature for me. Who will take my ideas and turn them into a manuscript with depth and… structure.' There's a pause before that last word comes out, possibly a delay in the text-to-speech software I suspect they're using, although it felt like they were searching for the right words. I can't help but wonder why they don't want to use their own voice? Are they famous? Famous people sometimes have ghost-writers, and it would make sense that they don't want me to see their face too, but I would have expected Professor Jarvis to tell me if that was the case.

'Do you mean you wish for me to help with the narrative, or do you already know how you want that to be? Do you already have your plot planned out or do you wish for help with that, too?' I say, recalling everything I researched on ghost-writing. If I know what Dr B's expectations are, it should help me give the right responses to the rest of his questions. I hope.

'I have a brief plot that needs further development, but I must say, you ask a lot of questions. I wonder, do you feel like you're interviewing me as much as I'm interviewing you?'

Again, a flush warms my cheeks, although I'm starting to wonder if that's their aim – to make me feel uncomfortable. As far as first impressions go, they're not making a great one, yet I suppose if you can afford the type of money this ghost-writing project pays, then you don't care what menial people like me think about you.

'I realise that this is you interviewing me,' I say. 'Very much so. But from what I have gathered, this is often a very collaborative process.'

'And you want to make sure I'm a person you can collaborate with?' The robotic sounds come out with no trace of humour or anger, just as an unreadable string of syllables. 'I will certainly try to be, if this works out, but now it is time for me to ask my questions. To learn about you. I assume that is agreeable?'

'Yes, absolutely. I didn't have a chance to send through a CV, but if you'd like—'

'They won't be that type of question. I need to know what you are like as a person; that is what matters to me. Like you, I need to know that I am working with a person I can collaborate with and who will express my ideas freely. Francesca – do you like to be called Francesca to start with? What about Frankie, or Franny? Fran, even?'

I let out an involuntary shudder at the sound of the name Franny. That was what my dad used to call me. Franny or Fran Fran. Never ever Frankie or Francesca, which is why I make sure that those are always the names people address me by now.

Whether or not he was guilty of what the police said he did doesn't change the fact that Franny is reserved for him.

'Francesca or Frankie is fine,' I say. 'I don't mind either.'

'Then I shall go for Francesca. Well, Francesca, can you tell me what in your life you are most proud of?'

'What I'm most proud of? You mean in terms of my literary accomplishments?'

'No, no, no, you as a person, as a human being. What are you most proud of? Have you fundraised thousands for charity? Climbed a mountain, performed cello on an international stage? Of course, if your literary accomplishments are the thing you are most proud of, then by all means, say those.'

The answer requires some contemplation. I had expected to be asked about my writing goals, writing accomplishments, favourite novels, authors that inspire me – that type of thing. I didn't think I'd be asked to talk about me as a person. The suggestions they have made, like climbing mountains and fundraising, make me feel unusually inadequate.

'This seems to be causing you some difficulty.' Dr B's voice cuts through my thoughts. 'How long does it take to think up some cliché answer, like getting into a top university or being invited to a lucrative job with so little experience? That's what you were going to say, isn't it? Something like that?'

There is no tone to the voice, but I don't need it to know they're trying to rile me, although I ignore it. They want an answer that nobody else has given before? Well, that's what I'll give them.

'What I'm most proud of is that I picked myself up again after a tragedy that would ruin most people. That I haven't let my past dictate my future. That I have a real life, worth living, when for years, I thought that would be beyond me.'

I've barely finished when their next question comes through.

'What was this tragedy that you speak of? If you feel comfortable in telling me about it, of course?'

I don't. I never feel comfortable talking about it. Some people would say I compartmentalise well, but I'd say I've blocked it out. I've put up a wall so high and thick that I almost pretend it never happened other than those handfuls of times a year when I visit my mother's grave. But as much as I don't want to tell anyone else, I know how much money is at stake right now. And it's not like I have to give Dr B everything, just enough for them to think they're getting a deeper insight into my mind, because that's obviously what they're after.

'My parents died when I was eighteen,' I start. I know I'm missing some of the most important elements of the story, but I'm not giving them that. I'm giving them just enough to think I'm disclosing it all. 'When they died, I was very much alone. No family. No close friends. I lost the most important people in the world to me and unsurprisingly fell into a pit so consumed with grief that for years, I didn't think it would be possible to climb out. But I did. I climbed out of it by myself.' I feel a pang of guilt as I say these words. Gloria played the biggest part in pulling me out of that pit and without her, I might still be there, but I can't let her into my head right now. Not when I need this. 'The fact that I keep going and that people I see on a day-to-day basis don't know this about me, that's the thing I'm most proud of.'

For a second, I think I should stop there, but then an image of Duncan rises in my mind. One where he tells me every day how much he loves me and how proud he is of me. His pride is mine, and I deserve to share that.

'I guess I'm proud of having a heart still capable of loving too. Of knowing that I'm building an incredible future, and that I'm even thinking about the future when, for years, every breath felt like agony. I am most proud of knowing my legacy will not be dictated by my past. That's what I'm most proud of.'

When I sit back in my seat, I'm surprised to find I'm almost out of breath. My heart is hammering against my ribs so hard, it's causing a rush of blood to throb behind my temples. And for a minute, they are the only sounds I can hear. My body. My breaths. Beyond them is absolute silence. Silence that stretches and stretches as it wraps a tension around my body.

Dr B has not said a word. I stare at the screen, waiting for them to speak. To say how sorry they are that I had to suffer such loss, or reinforce how proud I should be of myself, but still there's nothing at all, and for a moment, I wonder if they are still there. But as I clear my throat and prepare to say something, the tinny, robotic voice rattles through my speakers.

'Fine. Now tell me what you're most ashamed of.'

3

Any doubts I had about this being an abnormal interview have been erased. When the hell did anybody ever ask you to talk about what you are most ashamed of? The surge of adrenaline from my last answer has left my breath quickened, though I respond to the question almost immediately.

'I suppose it would be the depression I fell into after my parents' deaths.'

'Bullshit.'

The answer causes me to flinch in surprise.

'Sorry?'

'I call bullshit on that. You just told me how you're most proud of picking yourself up again. Your shame can't come from the antithesis of that, because you know that you were well within your right to face depression. I'm sure with what you went through, it would be almost expected, and you would never think badly of another for suffering that, so I do not believe you would be ashamed of yourself. So like I say, bullshit. What are you actually most ashamed of?'

I can feel my jaw hanging open as I stare at the screen.

'I can assure you that's the case.'

'Well, I assure you, I think that's bull. Give me something real. Show me how much you want this. Show me your dark side.'

My jaw is still slack, but I still manage to scoff.

It's clear now that this entire interview has been a game. Probably the same game they've played with all the other interviewees, and I'm done with it. They've been trying to rile me, and they've succeeded.

'Right now, the thing I'm most ashamed of is actually believing that this was a genuine interview. That you were someone who was keen on creating a piece of literary work, rather than just tormenting people for your own entertainment. I'm ashamed that I actually lost hours of my life being nervous about some sick prank to fulfil your own twisted desires. That, I promise you, is the very depth of my shame. Thank you for your time, but I'm done here.'

I don't even bother switching off the screen; I just slam the laptop lid closed, and for a second, I stay there, my heart pounding.

I feel physically sick. Whoever this Dr B is, they are not somebody I want in my life. My shame? There is nobody in the world who knows the truth of my shame, because I won't even admit it to myself. I'm sure as hell not going to let a stranger know the thoughts that whir through my mind in the depths of my darkest hours. Not a freaking chance.

With my eyes closed, I draw in several deep breaths. I won't let somebody like this get to me. I've been through far too much for that to be the case.

But Dr B has got under my skin. The questions. The voice. The anonymity. It's all a play designed to disturb whoever they're talking to, and I'm embarrassed at how well it worked on me. They could offer me twice the pay and I would still run a mile.

A flicker of guilt sparks within me. Duncan was so optimistic. He had so much faith in me, and now I'm going to have to tell him what I did. How I hung up in anger. I'm sure he'll see the truth, though, that I was never actually in with a chance of getting the job and earning this money.

My pulse has just about returned to normal, but the unease of the situation has left me not wanting to be on my own. Unfortunately, Duncan is gigging and won't be home until close to midnight. I can't even stay in the library that much longer, what with it closing in just under an hour. Which means I have to find another way to deal with this anxiety.

As I contemplate my options for the night, I can't help but be even more annoyed. It was a dodgy Zoom call. That was all. I should have forgotten it already. After all, I went back to my parents' house only three weeks after the incident. I would probably still be there if Gloria and Duncan hadn't persuaded me that I needed to move on with my life. As I think back to those days, a pang of sadness hits me. I really had assumed Gloria would be the one friend who would be in my life forever. So many left me after the incident, either because of what happened or because of how I refused to believe the police report and my dad's guilt. It was cut and dry in their minds. Murder-suicide. But they didn't know my father. They didn't understand he'd never do something like that. Part of me thought I'd never trust anyone again. But then Gloria turned up. She restored just a tiny sliver of the faith I had in humanity. And if it hadn't been for Duncan, she would've destroyed all of that again.

With a short breath in, I try to shake Gloria from my mind and fire off a message to Heidi.

> Thinking of going to watch Duncan at his gig. Fancy coming with me?

I don't go out much. I can probably count the number of times I've actually socialised over the past year on one hand. But I need a drink, and I don't want to do it alone at home, with Phil playing his computer games so loudly in the living room that I have to wear earplugs just to hear myself think.

The message goes through but remains unread. I shouldn't be surprised. Heidi books up her weekends months in advance. She calls it 'the burden of an influencer lifestyle', saying that it stops her from doing anything spontaneous. But we both know she's not going to quit anytime soon, or possibly ever. And why should she? If she does finally finish the novel she's been talking about writing for the last five years, she's got a ready, waiting audience.

Of course, I could have an audience too if I told people about my past. If they knew who I was, I'm sure there'd be plenty of people wanting to read a book by a woman whose father supposedly killed her mother and left her alone to come out the other side of the tragedy. But I have no intention of using my past as leverage for my future.

I move from the messages on my phone to the dial screen. There's a good chance that Heidi will happily invite me along to wherever she is, but as I scroll down my contacts list to her name, my eyes stop on the one above it. Gloria.

It's been over a year since I stopped trying. Since I gave up trying to make her talk to me. To make her explain why she suddenly no longer wanted to be a part of my life. I went through the emotions of grief at her loss almost as keenly as I had done with my parents, but unlike with them, I eventually came to a conclusion: if she didn't want to be in my life, then I should just accept that and move on with mine. I truly thought I was over her. Over the loss of the friendship. But as I stare at her name, my heart twists and tightens, and before I can stop myself, I hit dial.

4

You hear the saying 'it's a slippery slope' all the time, don't you? With things like depression or addiction. Alcohol or anxiety. With anything that's remotely negative, people are ready to spurt that saying. But for me, it wasn't. No, there was no smooth sliding descent for me. It was a plummet. One drop straight down. My parents' death rocked everything. People's refusal to believe that someone else might have been responsible. The therapist I saw said that my denial was due to my guilt.

During my younger years, Mum and I were inseparable, probably because of how much time my father spent away for work. It's unsurprising that she was my original go-to person for so long. But then, around the age of twelve or thirteen, that changed.

It wasn't that I no longer loved my mother. I did. I adored her. But there was something so special about my father. I'm sure our constant separation played a part in the rose-tinted glasses through which I viewed him. While he continued to spend weeks away on long-haul trips, the closeness that I had once adored with my mother frustrated me. Her mannerisms and foibles would niggle and grate on me. And mine on her. It was never anything major. Just the normal gripes of a mother and a teenage daughter, compounded by how much time we spent together. She was the one who had to tell me to tidy my room, who had to get me up in the morning and at night, force me into bed when I still wanted to stay up. I wasn't a bad kid. Far from it. But she was still the only one who had to parent. He was the one who would sweep in, like the sun, and make me feel like I was some sparkling, golden, magical treasure that he couldn't live without.

I sometimes wonder if she died thinking he was my favourite. If she took that bullet to the stomach – whoever fired it – believing that I loved my father more than her. I hope to God she didn't.

Their deaths were only part of what I had to suffer. There was the police. The news crews. Paying off my father's debt and discovering that my inheritance was little more than a few thousand pounds. I had to endure being alone. Truly alone.

And the thing is, with a slope, there's some chance of climbing out. You see it at the play park all the time. The rebelling children who stubbornly claw their way up metal slides, despite their parents' protests. Or the hikers who use their poles to tackle the steepest terrain that normal folk like me would shun. But a sheer cliff face, like the one I was pushed off after my mother's murder? There's no way you can claw your way out of something that vertical. It's just not possible. You need another person either to throw down the rope or to yank you out of the abyss. You can't do it on your own. But for nearly a year, I didn't have anyone. No one I trusted to hold the ladder steady enough that I could step onto that first rung.

But then Gloria showed up.

Moving was normal for me growing up. By the time I was sixteen, I'd lived in nine different houses, and every time we got a new place, my dad would let me decorate my room in whatever style I wanted, regardless of what the landlord said. Rainbow-coloured walls, a mural of Aslan. I even went dark red during my very brief goth phase. It didn't matter. Whatever I wanted, he made sure I had it. He would smooth it over later.

I know a lot of his behaviour was because of guilt, of course. It was his job making us move constantly, after all. He wasn't just an average long-haul driver; he helped set up new depots around the country, and that meant taking us with him. Looking back, my childhood lacked consistency. I got good at forming friendships fast, but there was never much depth to them, and while my birthday parties were often lavish affairs, where every person in the class was invited, sometimes I'd only been at the school a few weeks and didn't even know everyone's name by that point.

Secondary school was harder still. Cliques were tougher to get into and nastier when they broke. So I focused on my schoolwork, hid away in books, and concentrated on reaching my goal of being a great writer. That was what I wanted. To write stories like the ones that I stayed up at night for, reading under the covers until my eyesight blurred. Stories like the ones my mum and dad would pile up on their bedside cabinets to read. I wanted to write mystery stories, fantastical stories, maybe even romance. I didn't care. All I knew was that it was my mission in life to write. A mission that I abandoned the moment they died, and I might never have thought of again had Gloria not come into my life.

My parents had been dead for eleven months, and the local papers had just about stopped hounding me – other than the occasional 'anniversary pieces' that came out at almost monthly intervals. It probably helped that I gave them nothing, and there was no one else to go to in the hope of finding sordid titbits about my parents. We had only been in the Suffolk village for two years when they died – just long enough for me to do my A levels – and I had nowhere else to go. Literally. No aunts and uncles. No godparents. One good friend of my mother's from when we lived in Southampton offered to put me up, but I could tell it was a hollow offer. She had three of her own children, all under thirteen. There was no way she wanted to add an orphan of horrific circumstances to that situation. Not unless her plan was to use me as a live-in babysitter. Besides, the landlord was happy to keep me in the house at minimal rent – it wasn't like he could get anyone else in, although he did sort out the repaint at no cost to me.

I don't know how I planned to live my life, or if I even intended to keep living it at all, but then one day, she came knocking on my door.

'You live in this house by yourself, right? You've got an empty double bedroom. Any chance you want to sublet it?'

Sublet my parents' bedroom? I actually laughed at this curly-haired woman who didn't look much older than me as she stood on my doorstep with so much confidence.

'You don't want to live here,' I said. 'Believe me.'

'Because your dad killed your mum downstairs, yeah, I know. I went into the estate agents, told them my budget, and they laughed. Then someone suggested I see if you were in the market for a housemate. They gave me the landlord's number, but I figured I should check the place out for myself. See if I get bad vibes or anything. So?'

'So?'

'So can I check it out? I don't have much stuff. This is it.' She pointed to the heavy rucksack on her back as I stepped to the side, still not sure what I was doing as I let her walk through the hallway and into the living room.

'Nice television. Sofa looks comfy.'

She slung her bag off her back and dropped down onto the chair as I stared at the TV screen and the thick layer of dust that covered it.

'I'd need to have this seat. Or we could move the chairs. I just hate it when you get a reflection on the screen, don't you?'

'I... I'm not... It doesn't bother me. And he didn't kill her. The police just didn't bother looking into anyone else. They were lazy.'

Her eyes moved from the room to meet mine, and it felt for the first time like someone was actually listening to me. 'That's shit. Really shit,' she said, before shrugging. 'Well, I'm a very average cook, but I can use a jar of sauce if you fancy alternating meals. Actually, cooking for you might be a good idea. Otherwise, I'll just live off cheese toasties.'

'I like cheese toasties,' I said, still unsure whether the strong impression I was getting of this girl was positive or negative.

'Me too, maybe too much. But we could have one cheese toastie night a week. Maybe with a movie, if you like films. But not romcoms. I hate romcoms.'

And just like that, I had a roommate.

5

Her name is at the top of the screen, with 'Calling...' written below it. I can feel the air quivering in my lungs as I hold it tightly, like I'm not sure what might happen if I allow myself to breathe.

Even as I stare at the phone, I'm not expecting the call to go through. Maybe it'll give a long, strange dial tone, like she's abroad. Maybe it'll do nothing at all. Just go dead as she hangs up on me the way she has done dozens of times before. Or maybe an electronic voice will tell me that this number is no longer in use. There are numerous options for what could happen, and I'm ready to hang up, but before I do, an unexpected noise takes me by surprise. It's ringing. A normal ringtone is chiming from the speakers.

Each ring causes my pulse to hitch higher. I can't remember the last time I got this close to speaking to her, and the thought that she might pick up causes a new fear to flood me. What am I going to say? 'I'm pleased you're alive'? 'Where the hell have you been?' 'Why the fuck did you leave the way you did?'

My heart is rising higher and higher in my throat, making my breaths grow more and more shallow. Any second now, I'm going to be sent to voicemail. I'm certain of it. And I'm not humiliating myself by leaving another message that she won't bother listening to. That habit died months ago. Besides, I've suffered enough humiliation for one night. I hover my thumb above the end call button, only for the ringing to stop.

'Frankie?'

It takes me a second to realise that it's actually her. It's actually Gloria. Tears prick the backs of my eyes.

'Gloria. I didn't think you'd answer,' I say.

'I... I know... I don't think I should have.'

Her voice sounds timid. Strange. And yet unmistakably Gloria.

'I'm glad you did. It's good to hear your voice.'

A pause follows my words. One that extends so long, I have to check my phone to make sure she hasn't hung up. When she speaks again, her words have a far harsher timbre.

'Why are you calling me?'

The lump that was rising in my throat is now blocking it entirely as I struggle to respond.

'I... I just wanted to hear how you were. I've missed you.'

Again, she doesn't respond immediately, but it's not entirely silent. There's a slight rattle. A sniffing, perhaps.

'Gloria, are you okay? You can talk to me; you know that, right?'

There is no mistaking it. The sound that comes through next is a sob. A definite sob. My heart surges. I knew. I knew she wouldn't leave me so cruelly if there hadn't been a reason for it. Something that made her believe she had to stay away from me.

'Gloria, I can help you. You know that, don't you? Duncan and I can help you.'

'No!' Her voice is sharp. Almost a shout. 'It's not safe, okay?

We're not safe. Frankie, you need to watch out. He's... He's... It's not... I can't—'

'Gloria?'

'I'm sorry.'

A second later, the line goes dead.

6

Less than an hour ago, I felt full of optimism. Well, as full as optimism as I ever get. Of course there were lingering doubts as I didn't really expect to get the Dr B job when he had already turned down professional writers, but there was hope, and for someone who's been through the type of shit I've been through, you don't take that for granted. It felt like I was about to turn a massive corner in my life, professionally, yes, but also personally. The ghost-writing was going to be that final step I needed to move away from my past. But now I've voluntarily slipped myself back into it.

My hands are trembling as I stare at the blank phone screen. Gloria sounded scared. That wasn't just my imagination, was it? But if that was the case, why wouldn't she talk to me? And what did she mean about it not being safe? Gloria never shared much about her past. She used to spend weekends away, York, London, various places across the country visiting friends and family, and that happened more and more when Duncan and I got together, but she never used to share any photos, or even have a social media account for other people to tag her in. She was about 'the moment'. That was what she would say. Now, though, I'm wondering if it was something else. Maybe she didn't want people to know what she was up to for a reason.

I close my eyes, trying to imagine the response Duncan will give me when I tell him about my evening. He'd agree with me about Dr B being some sick, twisted bastard, that's for sure. And he'll likely say I was crazy for trying to contact Gloria.

She might be the reason that he and I found each other, and he knows everything she did for me, like getting me an online job tutoring so I could earn some money and persuading me to come here and do the degree I've always dreamt of – which meant finally leaving my parents' home and admitting I'd never get the answers I craved – but I know he'll never forgive her for hurting me the way she did. For packing up and leaving. It's safe to say his comment about Gloria isn't likely to be positive.

Duncan always thought she was jealous of our relationship and that was why she left like that, but if that was the case then why did she stay for so long? He also suggested she's the type of person who enjoys rescuing people, and once I didn't need rescuing, I wasn't that interesting to her any more. I don't know why she behaved the way she did, but whatever the reason, it made me angry. Really angry. She knew the only people who truly mattered to me had been ripped from my life and then, when I'd finally put some of my pieces back together, she did the same thing. But while my anger transformed into sadness, Duncan's has refused to fade.

'Do not get pulled in by her.' That's what he'd say to me. 'You are making something of your life here. We are making something of our lives. It's the future we should be thinking about, not our past.'

I try to hear the words in his voice and try to make them sink in, but it doesn't work. I need to speak to him, or at the very least see him, and I don't want to wait until gone midnight to do that, which leaves me only one option. I guess I'm going to his gig alone.

7

I'm halfway across London when I start regretting my choice to go and watch Duncan perform. I probably should have given up and gone home when I realised I didn't actually know where the gig was. Duncan has several regular spots with a couple of different bands across the city, and I was half sure this was one of those, but I had to check on the location app to see where his phone was. We don't have the app because we don't trust each other. It's mainly used for when I want to see if Duncan's on the way home, or when I've said I'm going to work late in the library and he wants to check I'm still there without disturbing my work.

There are closures on several of the Underground lines, and even on those that are running, my timing is terrible, meaning I miss the connections. As such, it's taking me far longer to get there than I thought, and I'll be lucky if I catch the last twenty minutes of their set. That's not the only reason I wish I'd gone straight home, though. I've felt this unnatural unease during the journey. Like somebody's watching me. Following me, even. It's just paranoia, I know that. I went through the same thing after my parents' death, when I was trying to convince the police that my father wasn't guilty and was seeing every person I passed as a suspect. That's why I couldn't move out and start over somewhere new, the way everyone expected me to. The way most people do when tragedy strikes, and they want to get as far away from the scene of the crime as possible. For me, it was different.

It was almost like if I stayed in the house long enough, I'd find the truth. That maybe the person who was responsible for their murders would return and I would finally have the evidence I needed to clear my father's name. I didn't want to leave until I had the answers, even though I knew the chance of ever knowing what happened in those last minutes of their lives was almost zero. There's a good chance I would have stayed in that house forever, and I think Gloria knew that. I suspect that was why around eighteen months after she moved in, she suggested I go to the group grief counselling sessions at the next village across. Grief counselling sessions where I met Duncan.

His situation couldn't have been more different from mine. He'd lost his younger brother a year before to a drunk driver, and he'd had to hold it all together for the sake of his parents. To say they struggled with the death would be a massive understatement. Even now, they refuse to say his brother's name. Refuse to talk about him or even acknowledge he existed. I've been for dinner with them numerous times over the years, and before each one, Duncan reminds me explicitly not to bring up his brother's name. It's tough for him, still having to play that role when all he wants to do is celebrate the life of a person he loved.

Those sessions were the first time he openly let himself show just how broken he was, and how he wished he could have the space to just grieve and break down. Week after week, we shared our experiences, first with the group and then more and more just to one another. Text messages, telephone calls, late-night video chats, though often those were less chatting and more me listening to him practise his guitar for some gig or another. In our collective pain, we discovered that our broken pieces fitted together perfectly. Like Kintsugi, the Japanese art of broken pottery. We filled the gaps in us with something lovely, though neither of us wanted to admit it at first.

It was over a year before we finally started dating – which is probably good as it meant I kept going to the grief counselling sessions, even though it was just to see him. After that, we were inseparable. At least we wanted to be, but for me, that posed a new challenge. He was – and still is – trying to make it as a musician, which means that if I want to see him, I have to shun the reclusive cloak that I've been wearing so comfortably since my parents' deaths and head out to bars and clubs to watch him perform. Thankfully, I quickly learned that listening to him play doesn't have to involve speaking to anyone and now, I'm a pro at sitting at a bar, watching his band and harbouring a scowl potent enough to deter any unwanted attention.

As I get off at the final Tube station, I notice someone on the other side of the platform. They're wearing a black hoodie, with the hood over their head. Normally, I wouldn't think twice about someone dressed like that, but something about their stance makes me do a double take. Are they staring at me? I can't tell, given that their face is hidden in the shadows.

I slow my pace and drop back so I'm between a group of middle-aged couples. A second later, the figure has passed us and I breathe a sigh of relief, though I'm not entirely sure why. I don't actually believe I'm in any danger, do I? I can't answer that. All I know is the sooner I get to Duncan, the better.

8

I squeeze my way through the bar to the front of the room. The band has just got offstage, and as always, there's a small crowd gathered around them. Mostly student-aged girls. One of them is talking to Duncan. She keeps throwing her head back and laughing while twirling her hair. I don't think I've ever seen somebody twiddle their hair as much as she is doing, and the way she's fluttering her false eyelashes is making me dizzy. I can tell from the glazed look in his eyes and the forced smile on his lips that Duncan really doesn't want to be having this conversation, but he is way too polite to tell her to get lost. For a moment, I just watch them. I don't blame girls like her for chancing their luck. He's an attractive guy and if he was single, she would have found herself a catch. Thankfully, I trust him explicitly, and that's something I never thought I'd say about anyone after I lost my mum and dad.

I go to move towards them, when Duncan spots me. His eyes suddenly brighten in a way that makes my heart flutter.

'Sorry,' he says, putting a hand on the girl's shoulder to move her to the side so he can cross towards me. 'You have a great night, all right?'

A moment later, he's standing in front of me with his hands on my waist, kissing me gently on the lips. When he breaks away, his smile is so broad, it's impossible not to reciprocate.

'Well, this is a very welcome surprise. I didn't expect to see you here. How did it go? You blew them away, right?'

'I'm not sure I'd say that,' I say. 'It was strange. And not in a good way. It was freaky.'

'Freaky how?'

I raise my eyebrows, implying there's a lot to digest here. 'Well, they asked me what I was most ashamed of, and swore at me when they didn't like the answer I gave.'

'What?' His eyes bug out.

'Yup. Oh, and they didn't show their face, spoke through a computer, and honestly creeped me out.'

Duncan grimaces. 'That doesn't sound good.'

'No.' I let out a long sigh. 'I'm sorry, I know the money would have been amazing, but I can't—'

'Hey, no,' he says, shaking his head to stop me. 'You don't need to apologise. It's fine. And there'll be other jobs like this that come up, right? Ones where the client isn't so odd?'

'Fingers crossed,' I say.

I don't know how Duncan does it. I know he must be disappointed and yet he manages to hide it so well, you'd never know. Just another of his endless talents, I guess. 'You okay to hang around here for a bit? We need to find the manager to get paid and pack all the gear away. It'll probably be about another twenty minutes.'

'Sure, I'll just grab a drink at the bar.'

'Thank you. Love you.'

A moment later, he walks away, and I find an empty seat. All the bar staff are busy taking orders, and I don't try to make my presence known. I'm not that bothered with getting a drink. I'm happy just scrolling on my phone while I wait for Duncan to be done, yet when I pull it out of my pocket, something on the lock screen causes me to start.

'You've got to be kidding me.'

9

Duncan and I are back home together, staring at the laptop. I didn't trust that the banking app on my phone was correct and so I opened it on the computer, but the numbers are saying the same. Apparently I have £5,283.26 in my account. Exactly £5,000 more than was there when I checked it yesterday. And the deposit has come directly from the ghost-writing company. I struggle to say anything. My heart is beating far too fast to be healthy. The only thing I know about Dr B is that they're not someone I want to work with, but by the looks of things, they feel differently.

'I don't understand how they can have paid you,' Duncan says. 'You said the person was a creep. That you didn't get the job?'

'I didn't get offered the job,' I say. 'I hung up on them. It all got too weird.' Although right now, it feels like it's getting even weirder.

'But that makes no sense. You must've signed something. They've got your bank details.'

'I signed the form they said I needed to in order to be considered for an interview. I put my bank details on that, but I assumed they'd only be used if I actually got the job.'

'Right,' Duncan says, drawing out the word longer than feels natural. 'Did you actually read the full contract?'

'Most of it.' As I say the words out loud, I realise it was probably a mistake. Give me a five hundred-page novel, and I can devour it in a matter of days. But contracts and formal jargon – that's not my thing. I'm one of those people who clicks 'yes' on the terms and conditions without scrolling past the first page. For all I know, I've promised my soul to a dozen different satanic beings. And I don't just mean the data miners.

'Okay, well, I guess we need to read through that contract then,' Duncan says, 'and work out where we go from there.'

'I'll make the coffees.' I don't care that it's near midnight. I want this sorted as quickly as possible.

Twenty minutes later, Duncan has scoured the PDF, highlighting several sections that I definitely should've read before I signed at the bottom.

'It says here that by agreeing to interview for a position, you are agreeing to accept that position should the client wish to offer it to you,' he explains.

'I don't have a choice?' My throat tightens.

'Not once you've agreed to interview. Judging from this, an abstract overview of what the project is is sent out to ghost-writers, at which point, they decide if they want to proceed.'

'Okay, but I didn't get that. Is that good? That means it can't be binding, right? That means I can get out of it.'

'I'm not sure.' I can tell Duncan's taking his time to process it all. Something I should have probably done too. He draws in a long breath. 'Do you know what the book is about?'

'No. I don't have a clue. They could be expecting me to write anything.'

And after the disturbing manner of our interview, I don't expect they want some light, frilly romcom. The silence that settles between us isn't comfortable, it's concerned, and I feel an overwhelming urge to fill it.

'I get it. I should have known better than to sign a contract without reading it through properly. But it's too late for that now, so what do I do?' I consider my question only momentarily before I respond. 'Professor Jarvis will know, won't he? He's the one who put me forward for this. I'll just have to tell him I shouldn't have signed the contract without the brief.'

'There's no harm in trying.'

I know that tone in Duncan's voice. It means he doesn't think I'm going to be able to get out of this, but the thought of having another meeting with Dr B, even if it is just online, causes a chill to run down the length of my spine. First thing in the morning, I'm going to see Professor Jarvis. He's the one who got me into this. Now he can get me out of it.

10

I might be older than the average student, but I still stick to the stereotype of coming in as late as possible, then working into the early hours of the morning. Of course, I have a genuine reason for that. Duncan. If I left at the crack of dawn every day, I'd barely see him. But today, spending time with my boyfriend is the least of my concerns, and by seven-thirty, I'm heading onto campus to find Professor Jarvis. In his memoirs, he always talks about the early hours being his favourite time of day to write. How the quiet of the world allows his mind to be its loudest and most free. I'm hoping that's true and that he comes into the office well before his lectures start. If not, I'll just hang around until he arrives.

Professor Jarvis is a veritable 'who's who' in the publishing world. His résumé is insane; he's been nominated for awards twenty-four times – the same number of years as I've been alive – and has won fourteen of those accolades. He's had his books turned into radio dramatisations and feature films, and ten years ago, he took on a stint as the host of 'Hooked on Books', the popular radio book club, and the ratings were the highest they had ever been. However, he quit only six months after starting because of family issues – real family issues, not the made-up kind that people of his stature sometimes claim when they want out. His wife was sick and passed away about a year later. Many thought he'd never write again. After all, he frequently referred to Isabella as his muse. But rather than proving the cynics right, he became more prolific and more heartfelt, pouring his loss into every word he wrote. His pain is tangible in every sentence and paragraph. The turmoil and despair so clear that reading his words feels like you are watching a film of a man falling apart in front of your eyes. Those pieces he wrote after Isabella died were the first short stories I read by him. After that, I went on a binge. I started with his most well-known books, then the lesser-known yet award-winning ones, and even hunted down his early works that were out of print. Pieces that nobody really talked about. In each one, I found something new. I found bits of voice, prose, or dialogue that made me hold my breath and clutch those patterns of ink on paper so close to my heart that I felt I could become one with them. And it all became even more poignant after my own family's deaths.

It's weird to think I could almost have been working with him if I'd taken on this ghost-writing role, but that's not going to happen now. Not with the Dr B job, at least. The sooner he can help me get out of this situation, the better.

There are several floors' worth of corridors dedicated solely to the English faculty lecturers, and their rooms are grouped according to their specialties. Professor Jarvis is on the third floor amongst the general literary writers.

When I get to his room, the door is shut. It's not a great sign, but it is early, and most lecturers keep their doors shut.

With my speech already prepared in my head, I knock once and listen for a noise from inside. It's muffled; I assume that's because he's got his head down in a book, paper, or laptop. As such, I don't knock again before I turn the handle and open the door. A millisecond later, my hand flies to my mouth.

11

I don't know how long I stand there, or why I don't turn around and close the door behind me. It's a shock, I guess. Shock not so much at what I'm seeing, but who I'm seeing there lying across Professor Jarvis's desk, only half dressed.

'Shit, shit.'

Heidi's voice brings me back to the moment and snaps me out of my daze. For a split second, though, my feet still struggle to catch up, and I stay there, locked on the image of her trying to clip her bra.

'I'll come back, I'll come back,' I say, finally finding my voice. My leg muscles find it in themselves to move again too, and I swivel on the spot, race out of the room and close the door behind me. My throat has sealed shut, and my hands are trembling as I practically sprint down the corridor. When I reach the stairs, I stop, drop my hands onto my knees, and let out a long breath.

I don't know who I'm more surprised at: Heidi or Professor Jarvis. I know who I am more disappointed in, that's for sure. Fuck. He wasn't facing me, at least. That's something. All I saw of him was his back and his bare, white arse. It was Heidi I got to see full frontal as she rode on top of him. Maybe there's a chance that he didn't see it was me who came into the room. It could've been anybody. But Heidi will tell him. I'm sure she will. Besides, I spoke, and he knows who I am now. He knows my voice. Waves of nausea hit me; this doesn't feel good, not good at all.

I regain my breath and begin to descend the steps. I don't know how I'm going to handle this. But I know I need some time and space to figure it out. Yet almost as soon as I have that thought, I hear the footsteps padding up the hall behind me.

'Frankie?'

For a second, I just stand there, one foot hovering above the next step. I could just keep walking. She'd know I'd heard her and realise I don't want to speak to her, but I think I'm justified in acting that way. But then what? Ignore her for the next eighteen months of the degree? It's doable. I just don't know if it's what I want to do.

In a split-second decision, I turn around to face her.

Four steps above me, Heidi stands with flushed cheeks.

'Can we talk?' she says.

12

When I applied for my degree, I knew I wasn't going to university to make friends. I was there to learn as much as possible. I had no intention of being pulled into the life of these students, many of whom were still in their teens. My aim was to learn. To be the best. Of course, there was another reason I didn't want to mingle too much.

Newspapers that had once headlined with the news of my parents' horrific murder-suicide were now compost. Other tragedies had taken precedence in people's minds, but there was always that fear. That worry that people would know about my past. And even if people didn't, there were always going to be questions. Normal get-to-know-you questions like, 'Where are you from? What do your family do?' Telling them my parents died in a supposed murder-suicide didn't feel a great way to build friendships.

So, for the first two weeks, I spoke to no one. I moved between lectures silently. Picked the quietest place in the library to work and only spoke in seminars when questions were directed at me. I thought I was near enough invisible, though I was wrong. It was the third week, after a lecture on fantasy world-building, when Heidi accosted me on the way out of the campus.

'It's Frankie, isn't it?' she said. 'Frankie Crawford?'

I'd seen Heidi in my classes, always dressed immaculately, with designer bags and a brand-new computer and other things students can't normally afford. But I'd never spoken to her, and I'd definitely not told her my name.

'Why?' I asked.

'I was just checking. You are Frankie Crawford. Francesca Crawford?'

'Yes,' I said, as a ripple of tension rolled down me. 'Sorry, do I know you?'

At this, I expected her to introduce herself. Instead, she threw back her head and laughed.

'God, you have no idea how good it is to hear you say that. So many people start talking to me like we're best friends. Like they know everything about my life. Which, of course, they don't. They only get to see the snippets I want to share. But hey, I guess that's the life I signed up for.'

'Right,' I said, feeling the frown lines deepen in my forehead. I didn't have a clue what she was going on about.

'I'm Heidi Marland,' she said. 'The lifestyle influencer?'

'I'm afraid I don't know much about influencers,' I replied, still having no idea what was going on.

'Well, yes. That much is obvious. I knew I was going to like you. Come on, let's go get a coffee. Have you been to the new place that's at the end of the Fairfax Street? I did some promotional work for them and the manager always gives me a discount. Actually, he gives me everything I ask for. We should go there. My shout.'

I was torn. I'd never say no to free food, but this woman had way too much energy for my liking. Still, I needed to get to the bottom of how she knew my name, so I wasn't ready to end our conversation yet.

As we walked down the street, she talked non-stop, mainly about the course and writing. Apparently, she had dozens of articles already written and she, too, was in awe of Professor Jarvis, though we weren't yet in any of his classes. At no point did she allow me to get a word in edgeways, though just like she'd said, our sandwiches and drinks were all on the house. Although rather than eating hers when it came, she got her phone out and began moving the plates and cups around.

'I'm so sorry,' she said. 'This part takes forever.'

She was taking shots from every angle, standing up, crouching down and shifting everything around till the light was perfect. I was sure my drink would be stone cold by the time she was done, but thankfully, it was only a minute or so before she finally put the phone away.

'I like to come off campus whenever I can,' she said, biting into her sandwich. 'It just gives me a bit of room to breathe, you know. Especially given how often I'm recognised there. Not that I don't admire the younger students. You know they only take around 4 per cent of applicants they get for this course. That's amazing, right? I mean, we're the cream of the crop. Every person in that room is the cream of the crop.'

'Yes,' I said, feeling like I should respond. 'I guess they are.'

'Everyone there has had to show drive just to get a place.'

'I suppose you're right.'

I was building up confidence to ask her how she knew my name when her next words hit me with a blow so hard, they almost left me winded.

'But their drive is nothing compared to yours. Honestly. I have so much respect for you, putting yourself out there, after everything you went through with your parents. That's brave. Seriously brave.'

I felt the colour drain from my cheeks as she lifted her cup to her lips. I couldn't tell if it was to cover a smile or not, though now I know her better, I'm sure it was just bad timing.

'Don't worry, I'm not going to say anything to anyone. You deserve your privacy. And with someone in my line of work, I get that far more than you think.'

'How do you know?' I asked. My throat had constricted so tightly, I struggled to speak. 'Did you live locally? Do I know you from school?'

She shook her head.

'No. Not at all. Before I settled on lifestyle work, I tried out a couple of other social media ideas. I did a makeup channel for a while – which flopped – and then had a true-crime page. Your parents were one of the stories I looked at. Not that I posted anything on it. There wasn't that much story that I could tell. Other than your family kept themselves to themselves a bit and it was a major shock. But they'd seemed happy enough.'

'They were happy and if the police had done any actual detective work, they would have discovered he didn't do it.' The words flew out of my mouth with as much venom as I could muster. Disbelief and dread filled me. I had come here to get away from my past, but apparently that wasn't going to happen. With my appetite gone, I started to stand when Heidi reached across the table and grabbed my arm.

'I'm so sorry. I didn't mean to upset you,' she said. 'That was the last thing I wanted. What I wanted was for you to know that you have a person here if you need it. A friend. I didn't think it would be fair to pretend I didn't know who you were. I thought the truth would be the best option.'

Even without the perfectly applied eyeliner and false lashes, her eyes were enormous and I couldn't help but feel myself looking into them. Seeing the genuine guilt and upset she felt.

'I promise you, Frankie, I know what it's like to have to fight. To have people judge you for the only side of your life they see. I wanted to tell you that if you ever need someone to talk to or go for a drink with or just raid my wardrobe for new outfits, then I'm here. Seriously. The number of clothes I get given is sickening.' She quirked a smile.

Since then, over the last year, we've had coffee most weeks. She uses me as a reason to get away from the rest of the class as she insists they are all either fans or haters. The fact that someone could be oblivious to her isn't within her mindset.

13

Silent swells between us before Heidi finally clears her throat and speaks.

'Well, that was unfortunate timing,' she says, before walking down so she's level with me. A long, vertical window breaks up the wall in front of us and looks out over the lawn in front of the faculty. For a second, I shift my gaze and focus my attention there. I would give anything to be out there right now. Or rather, I would give anything to be anywhere other than in this exact situation, and yet Heidi is still standing next to me. When I turn to look at her, she offers the most apologetic smile I've ever seen her give.

'If it makes you feel any better, Ivor is furious that I didn't lock the door.'

'It doesn't,' I say through gritted teeth.

She lets out a slight laugh. 'No, sorry about that. I told him I did, but I thought it would be more exciting. Maybe that was an error in judgement.'

'I wouldn't say not locking the door was your only error here,'

I reply. My legs are still trembling, and the nausea tumbles through my body. But for the first time, I see a flicker of fear on Heidi's face.

'It's not what you think. We've tried to stop. We really have. And it's not like this is something he does. It's not. He's not like that. What we have is real. You won't say anything, will you?'

There's so much naivety in the air right now, it's cloying. I really didn't think Heidi was like that. Foolish enough to fall for the lies of an older man. But she's not the only naïve one. I genuinely thought Professor Jarvis was better than that. For a second, all I can do is stand there. Could I tell someone? Should I tell someone? Heidi isn't some inexperienced fresher, straight out of school. She's twenty-two. An adult. As dizzying as the concept is, the two are consenting adults.

As I consider how to reply, I turn my gaze back outside the window, only to see something that makes my heart lurch. Someone with dark, curly hair is turning in a circle, almost like they're lost or looking for someone. But it's their coat that holds my attention. Their multicoloured, knitted coat that I would recognise from a mile away. I squint, trying to see more clearly, but my pulse already knows what my head is refusing to accept. It's Gloria. Gloria is out there.

'Sorry, Heidi, I have to go,' I say, turning on the stairs, but she's on my heel and grabs me by the wrist, forcing me to turn around to face her.

'Please, you can't tell anyone. He'll get in trouble.'

'Fine,' I snap.

'Fine?'

'I won't say anything. I just need to go. Now.'

'Thank you,' she says as she releases me. 'Thank you so much. I should go tell Ivor. That was quite a shock we both had.'

I think she's expecting a response, but I don't have one for her. I'm too busy sprinting down the stairs. It was Gloria. I'm sure it was.

14

Three flights of stairs. That's how many I've got to go down, and I'm racing as fast as I can, but it's not quick enough. Any faster, though, and I know I'll fall flat on my face. Students are ambling their way into the building, blocking my route and slowing me down. When I finally reach the doorway, I stop to see if I can spot her, but when I don't, I race onto the lawn.

'Gloria? Gloria!'

I'm yelling at the top of my lungs. Turning around in a circle as I try to see in every direction at once. Several people turn to look at me, but I don't stop. Instead, I run towards them.

'Did you see a woman wearing a multicoloured coat?' I say. 'Curly hair? About twenty-seven.'

The group I've accosted all shake their heads and several back away slightly, looking at me like I've lost my mind.

'She was here just a minute ago,' I tell them, before realising I'm going to get nothing and move onto a different group. 'Did you see a woman with curly hair and a multicoloured coat? She was here a minute ago?'

Once again, there's nothing more than blank looks and apologies and after a minute, I stop asking and just focus on looking myself. The lawn's big, but it's fairly clear, with only a few trees to break up the aspect, but there are plenty of buildings she could have slipped between. Not to mention she could have headed back to the main road and off campus entirely.

'Are you okay? You look lost.'

I turn to face the voice. Standing in front of me is a young man. Young, but closer to my age than most of the students here. There's something familiar about him, but it's only when I see the two cups of coffee in his hand that I realise what it is. He's one of the PhD students. I'm pretty sure he works predominantly with Professor Jarvis, but I've seen him in Dr Ribero's lectures, sorting out the computer for her. Dr Ribero needs more help than the average lecturer with computers, and technology in general. I'm pretty sure she'd still use a blackboard if the university would let her.

With a sharp breath in, I shake my head, trying to bring myself back to reality.

'Sorry,' I say, offering the student a brief smile. 'Yes, everything is fine. I just thought I saw somebody.'

'Cool, well, I better get going.' He lifts up the two coffees to indicate he has places to be.

As he disappears, I stand there and look out at the road. I'm sure it was Gloria. I wouldn't bet my life on it, but something in my bones tells me it was her. First, she answers my phone call, then she's coming onto the campus of the university where she knows I study. Does she want to make amends, explain why she left, or maybe just clarify what the hell she was on about when she said we weren't safe? I've no idea, but finding Heidi and Professor Jarvis together, combined with the fact that I still need to get out of this Dr B job, I don't have the time or headspace to think about her right now.

One problem at a time. That's the most I can deal with.

15

I stay sitting outside until ten to nine, at which point I head in for my first lecture of the day, and to make my morning even worse, it's with Dr Ribero.

It's safe to say that poetry with Dr Ribero is my least favourite of the creative courses, and if I'm honest with myself, it's probably because I'm not as good at it as I want to be. Back in school, the teachers said I had a gift and it was my poetry that stood out, possibly more than the rest of my creative writing, but even back then, I knew the truth: I was faking it. Choosing pretty words and placing them in sentences with just enough ambiguity that people could imagine there was a deeper meaning hiding between the lines. Maybe there was, but it was never a conscious decision.

The first lecture we had with Dr Ribero, I knew she'd see straight through me.

'You can't fake good poetry,' she said. 'It's like taking a photograph of an oil painting. It doesn't matter that the same image is there; it's what creates the image that counts. The texture of the brushstrokes, the blending of the colours. The aroma that rises from the canvas as the light diffracts off the paint. It's about so much more than just the picture. Poetry is the same. Try to fake it and I will know.'

Her eyes locked onto me in that moment and it felt like she was seeing me for who I truly was. Seeing my inability. Seeing my fear of being caught out, and it terrified me.

When I came home from that lecture, my skin still buzzed with her words and I thought perhaps they were all I needed to transform my poetry. I believed that the moment our eyes locked had been the catalyst of something great within me. That it had ignited an ability to create something masterful in the form of poems. It hadn't.

Instead, if possible, my poetry became worse. Every word I wrote sounded more hollow. More distant and disconnected. More fraudulent.

'It sounds incredible to me,' Duncan said, as he read one piece I'd spent hours poring over, staring at it until my eyes began to sag, trying to improve it yet unable to find its failings.

'It's not,' I replied. 'It's average at best. I can't be average. Scholarship students aren't average and if I don't have my scholarship, I can't afford to be here, remember?'

He'd turned the laptop screen back to face me and locked his eyes on mine.

'You know you're just stuck in your head on this. Trust me, it's incredible and the lecturer will see that.'

'And if they don't?'

'Well, you get to drop poetry at the end of this semester, don't you?'

'Thank God.'

When I received the details about the scholarship, it said it would cover tuition for the full three years of my degree provided my attendance didn't slip under 98 per cent. It's currently sitting at ninety-nine, which is good enough, but I don't want them to look at my grades and suddenly decide they made a wrong call. As such, I've put more work into the nineteen lines of my latest poetry assignment than the last three thousand-word piece I had to do for the memoir module, but maybe that has as much to do with me not wanting to spend time thinking about my past as it does me trying to do the best I can for Professor Ribero.

I settle down in my seat, ready to start even though the lecture hall's only half full. My peers, like me, know that the first five minutes are going to involve her trying to get the projector to work by pulling out cables she doesn't need to touch and pressing combinations of buttons on her keyboard that send her computer into a frenzy. There's never any point arriving to this lecture on time. But I'm here, and I figure I can use the time to work on my current poem. I open up my laptop and scan through my work so far when my thoughts are suddenly interrupted.

'Francesca?'

Just from the tone, I know who it is. Professor Jarvis. Professor Jarvis has come into another lecture to find me after I walked in on him and Heidi. If I'd thought this day couldn't get any worse, I'm rapidly learning otherwise.

'Sorry to interrupt you, Ms Crawford, but can I please have a word?'

I'd love to say no. I'd love to tell him that I'm busy and make him stew for what he's done, but I need to ask him about Dr B. I can't get out of this without him. And so I give the only answer I can.

'Of course,' I say.

16

He looks different. That's the first thought that enters my mind. Professor Jarvis looks different now to how he does in lectures. He looks less confident, more tired. I guess that happens when you get caught having an affair with one of your students.

For a minute, I think he's going to lead me to his office and I'm really not sure I can cope with seeing that desk again so soon. Thankfully, he's walking towards the library, where he immediately heads into one of the study rooms. It's similar to the one where I had my meeting with Dr B last night, though how the hell that was less than twenty-four hours ago, I have no idea. So much has happened since then.

'You can take a seat or stay standing if you want – it's up to you,' he says. 'I don't mind.'

'Well, I—' I take a step in, but he already carries on talking.

'Did you know before?'

His words catch me by surprise. 'Sorry?'

'About Ms Maynard and myself? You're friends. Or so she says. Did she tell you about us?'

'No.' I'm genuinely confused by the unexpected turn this

meeting has taken. Does he really think this is why I wanted to see him? To call him out for sleeping with Heidi? I didn't know I was going to walk in on them. 'I swear, I didn't have a clue. She said nothing to me. And I shouldn't have come in without knocking. I heard a sound, and I thought—'

'I didn't know she was a student of mine.' For the second time, he cuts me off and this time, he carries on talking. 'And it wasn't like I sought her out. She was in a bar celebrating her birthday, and I... I was on my own. I figured she felt sorry for me, and that was why she asked me if I wanted to join them for a drink. Students don't go to that bar. It's too expensive. For most of them, at least. I guess you already know that Miss Maynard doesn't fit the normal student stereotype.' As he says this, a sad whimsy glazes his eyes. Almost as if he's genuinely fond of her. I'm about to say that I know Heidi deliberately avoids normal student hangouts and that I can believe their meeting was entirely coincidental, but before I can, he carries on talking. 'Maybe I shouldn't be hanging out at bars on a Friday night, but in my defence, being a widow is lonely. So damn lonely sometimes. We had no children, you see. When she died...' He stops and shakes his head, like he's suddenly realised he's sharing far more than he wants to. 'I need you to know that this isn't something I do. I'm not one of those lecturers, who... you know. I wouldn't. I'm just an idiot, I guess. An idiot who fell for the wrong girl. You could almost write it in a story, couldn't you?' he adds with a sad smile. 'One that probably has a tragic end.'

Against all my better judgement, I believe him. The way he speaks and the genuine feeling in his voice are almost identical to what I saw in Heidi only an hour ago.

'What you do with your private time is nothing to do with me,' I say. 'I came to see you because of the ghost-writing project you put me forward for.'

Instantly, his demeanour changes. It's not exactly relaxed, but it's definitely different.

'I got offered the job,' I say, finally getting to the reason I wanted to speak to him in the first place. 'The Dr B ghost-writing position?'

Professor Jarvis arches his eyebrows, and for a split second, there's something I can't read in his expression. But then it changes, and a broad, tense smile fills his face.

'Really? Well, congratulations.'

'I don't want it,' I say.

'I see. Why is that?'

I stop and draw a breath, trying to work out how to put what I want to say into words. My well-rehearsed speech is long forgotten. 'They don't use their voice,' I say. 'They put everything through a computer.'

'I had heard as much.'

'And they didn't show their face at all, and to be honest, they made me feel incredibly uncomfortable. Some of the questions they asked, were, well, bizarre.'

At this, his lips twist and his eyes become uncharacteristically skittish. 'Well, each of our clients is different, Francesca. You see, secrecy can be incredibly important. We often have politicians, members of MI5, government officials… They need to keep themselves anonymous. Perhaps I should've explained all this to you before I suggested you for the position.'

'Do you think?'

The fact that he isn't totally freaked out by this is a slight relief, but it still doesn't change how uncomfortable I felt in that interview.

'Look, what do I do? I didn't see a brief. It says in the contract I should see a brief. I didn't, so I don't have to accept the job, right? The rest of the contract can't count if that bit was neglected, can it?'

'Well, each of our clients works very differently. Several choose not to disclose a brief until they have found their writer and are beginning the process. They might just give one or two lines of detail. Especially if they're a celebrity.'

'You think that Dr B is a celebrity?' I say.

'Your guess is as good as mine, but they wouldn't have chosen you if they didn't think you were up to the task. But if you are that unhappy, I suppose you could get a lawyer.'

'A lawyer?' A slight scoff escapes my throat. I'm tempted to ask if he knows any students who can even afford lawyers, but instead, I stay silent and nod.

It's Professor Jarvis's turn to draw in a long breath. 'If it makes you feel any better, I don't believe they would've hired you if they weren't confident that you could do a good job. The same way I am. My advice to you would be: do what they say, and do it quickly. As soon as you finish the book, you'll be out of their lives, and they'll be out of yours.'

A lawyer is out of the question, so as far as I can see, I'm not left with any other option.

'I guess that's what I'll do then,' I say.

He nods. 'Well, with the job accepted, whether deliberately or not, a date for your first planning meeting will probably come through imminently, so I'm sure you'll find out all you need to know then.'

'Thank you.'

'And if you need any advice, you know I will be happy to help. If you are still comfortable in receiving guidance from me, that is.'

The hollowness in his voice makes me feel guilty, though I'm not sure why.

'Thank you, Professor Jarvis. I won't take up any more of your time.'

'It's quite all right. Perhaps you should start calling me Ivor now. That's what colleagues do.'

I smile, though it's tight-lipped and I'm sure he can tell.

'Thank you, Professor Jarvis,' I say.

Five minutes later and I'm on the phone with Duncan.

'There's no way out of it without paying for a lawyer and I can't imagine what that would cost us.'

'Okay, so what do you want to do?'

'Honestly?' I've already thought through that question, and I know exactly what the answer is. 'We might as well put the money to use. Let's find somewhere else to live.'

17

Professor Jarvis was spot on about the first meeting request coming through imminently. Within half an hour of leaving the library, I have a meeting link sent through for that night at 9 p.m., but rather than excitement, it's a new sense of anxiety that fills me, and it's not solely about the job and Dr B's way of making me feel uncomfortable.

9 p.m. is peak computer-game time for my housemate Phil and if he has friends around, this is when the tournaments really kick off. I normally only survive by wearing earplugs. That's not something I can do during a meeting. I could use the library, but that's not ideal either. Mondays are a lot busier, and the building gets locked up at 10 p.m. Given that I don't know how long this session with Dr B is going to last, I don't want to take the risk of being turfed out halfway through.

As far as I can see, there's only one option, which is to ask Heidi if I can use her place, and I really don't want to do that. Not just because of all this stuff with Professor Jarvis. I don't want to answer questions about what I'm doing or who I'm talking to. But I guess I don't have a choice. Besides, she probably already knows. I'm guessing pillow talk with the professor is the reason she sent me that good-luck text last night.

I find her between our next lectures, and as I probably could've predicted, she's over the moon about this development.

'I'll do us food,' she says. 'We can get takeaway? Or I can cook something if you like – you know I've mastered spanakopita.'

'It's fine,' I say. 'I'll eat with Duncan. I'll probably come round about ten minutes before, if that's all right.'

She looks a little disappointed by this, but I don't have time to pander to her ego. I've got enough to cope with.

'Sure,' she says with a strained smile on her face. 'Whatever works for you.'

'Great, I'll see you about quarter to nine then.'

When I get home that afternoon, Duncan has already got half a dozen rental properties for me to look at.

'What about this one?' he says, handing me his phone. 'Top floor, which means no noisy neighbours hammering above us, and the space – it's amazing.' It really is. It's a little further away from the university, but in a nice area of the city and even has a balcony that's big enough to have a table out on.

'That would be a dream,' I tell him.

'According to this, there are white goods, but other than that, it's unfurnished.'

'Unfurnished means we have to spend a lot of money on beds, sofas, a desk, TV.'

'Really, we don't need that much stuff,' he says. 'We can pick most of it up second-hand. I've already had a look on a load of local giveaway pages; there's plenty of stuff. I reckon we can get everything we need for eight hundred quid tops. I don't mind hunting it down.'

He offers me a grin, but there's a lot of worry niggling away at me. But the thought of spending the money Dr B has paid me causes my stomach to churn, and then there's the issue that we've never had that type of money before. Spending it the minute it enters our bank account doesn't feel like a great idea.

In my silence, Duncan reaches out and takes my hand.

'I know this is a big deal, Frankie. Personally, I think it's a no-brainer, but it's your advance. So it's your choice.'

I look at the view from the balcony again and consider sitting out there early in the morning with a cup of tea, watching the world unfold. Not that we actually own a kettle, either. No, that belongs to the house, so we'd have to buy that too. It's probably not going to be as cheap as Duncan thinks to move, but it's what we've been waiting for, and now we actually have the means to make it happen.

As I look at him, I can't stop the grin from rising on my cheeks.

'Okay, I guess we make a list of places we want to see and you go visit them on while I'm at lectures, if you're okay with that?'

'You don't want to come with me?'

'It's fine. I trust you. And I'm not going to have much free time any more. Not with this writing on top of everything else.'

His eyes sparkle as they dart down and look at the photos on the phone one more time. When they come back up, I swear there are tears glistening in them.

'We're going to do this, baby,' he says. 'Fingers crossed. By this time next week, we'll have a place of our own. And you know what, I'm sure this Dr B was messing with you. I bet they won't be half as bad tonight. Just wait and see.'

The mention of Dr B's name causes a tension to grip at my insides, but I try my hardest not to show it.

'Of course,' I say, almost certain I don't believe it.

18

I arrive at Heidi's at five to nine, acting all flustered to give the impression that I was accidentally running late. Actually, I just want to spend as little time with her as possible. I know if she gets me alone, she'll want to talk about her and the professor, and that's not something I can deal with.

'I'm really sorry,' I say. 'Duncan's going flat hunting tomorrow. We were looking through places together and time just ran away with me.'

'Flat hunting? That's amazing. You should absolutely have a place by yourself. Well, I've set you up in the spare room, and there's chilled water in there. I only had sparkling; I hope that's okay?'

'Sparkling's great,' I say as I head to the room, although, as I sit myself down, I can't help but wonder if there was something wrong with the tap.

'Just call me if you need me,' she says, poking her head around the door like she's some middle-aged aunt.

'I'm absolutely fine. I just need this to be private.' I pull out my headphones and place them straight on my head, hopefully reinforcing my point. I might not be able to stop her from listening in and hearing my half of the conversation, but at least I can stop her from hearing Dr B's, and that's probably the most important part.

'Of course, of course. Well, let me know when you're done. The wine's ready and waiting.'

As quickly as I can, I set up with a notebook beside me and a window open next to the video screen so that I can make notes on the computer if I decide that's easier. I wish I could record the meeting. If they say anything else inappropriate, I want to have evidence of it. I don't know what I'll do with that evidence, but I want it.

I have a list of questions I want to ask to kick things off. Things that are paramount to know before I start writing: genre, the story point of view, themes running through it, preference for style, and estimated word count, along with a few others, although I know it will depend on how much Dr B knows about writing as to how useful the answers I get back will be.

Bang on nine, I open up the call. Almost instantly, Dr B joins. There's no strange black background this time, though. They haven't even turned the camera on.

'Francesca, I'm so glad you agreed to take this position.'

It's a computerised voice again. Cold and emotionless. Immediately, the hairs on my arms rise, but I try to ignore the sensation. Professionalism. That's what I'm going for. I'm just going to get the job done.

'I'm very grateful that you wanted me to write your story for you, Dr B,' I say, 'and I'm really excited to get started, so I have a few questions that will help me make sure I know exactly what I'm doing, is that okay?'

There's a slight pause.

'Straight to business, aren't you?'

I don't bother feeling embarrassed by this comment. It's just part of a game I'm not planning on playing.

'Well, I'm sure that you want your work completed as quickly as possible, and the last thing I want to do is waste either of our time. I'm sure you understand that.'

'Yes, absolutely.'

'Great, well, I thought you'd want to start by just telling me about your vision for the book,' I say. 'If you're happy to do so.'

'Absolutely.'

The word comes through on its own, and I wait for the next response. For a minute, there is nothing. I clear my throat, wondering if perhaps they've forgotten to hit enter on their computer and that's why no electronic voice has reached me yet. But a moment later, the voice begins.

'It will be a multiple POV book,' they say. 'At least two running through the present tense, the others in the past.'

'Great. Multiple POV.' As I jot down my notes, I realise they said POV, rather than a point of view. Does that mean they've got some idea how writing works? I guess I'll find out as we go along.

'So, do you have all the characters already in your mind?' I ask.

'Some. There is a young woman I have a vision of. The others are coming to me more slowly. I will tell you now that there are going to be explicit scenes. Murder, assault – I assume those won't be a problem for you to write?'

It's a bold assumption to make, I feel. I'm pretty sure there are lots of people out there who wouldn't like to write about murder, but it's just writing to me. It's just words. A series of letters making sounds that our brains interpret in the manner that their experience and context tell them to. None of it is real. Unlike what I went through.

'That shouldn't be a problem,' I say. 'Do you have a character profile for this woman already? I find it useful to develop them when I'm writing a book. I won't necessarily use all the information that you give me explicitly, but creating a document with as much detail about the main characters as possible helps to ensure I'm showing the reader a fully rounded person.'

I'm basically parroting facts I've been told in countless lectures and courses since my interest in creative writing began. Flesh out your characters, so you know them before you start writing. That's what so many teachers have told me. But then there have also been those who say they never do them and certainly not before a first draft. That's when the characters finally speak to them. But somehow that feels a lot harder to pull off in a situation like this and I want all the information Dr B can give me.

'Do you want the physical attributes, interests, hobbies, things like that?' they say.

'Yes, that would be absolutely great. And as for the plot, personally, I always think it's helpful to know where you're going to end first. So we know what we're working towards. Do you have any idea how this book is going to end?'

'Oh yes, that I've always known.' The answer comes through immediately, and I'm about to ask them to give me a brief overview when they continue speaking anyway. 'It will end with deaths. Murder-suicide. That won't be a problem for you to deal with, will it? You know, given what happened to your parents.'

19

My hands are shaking and all the blood has drained from my face. I want to reach out and end the call. Better still, turn the entire computer off. But that's exactly what they're expecting me to do. It's probably what they want.

'I don't think—' I begin.

'I'm sorry.' The voice comes through before I can finish my sentence. 'I realise I overstepped the mark. Please understand, it was not my intention to make you feel uncomfortable. I research people. It is what I do before I decide to take them on to a project. It is not just you; I did it with every writer I considered working with. For example, Rupert Fitzherbert, the notable writer who interviewed for this role, was removed from a position in the very faculty you are studying a little over three years ago and has over twenty grand of gambling debt. I can also tell you that your own Professor Jarvis has been having an affair with a student for the past three months. The list goes on if you would like more examples?'

My throat has clamped shut and not just because of my parents. Rupert Fitzherbert is the most established modern writer of this region. If Dr B is telling the truth, why the hell would he have interviewed him and not given him the job? And as for Heidi and Professor Jarvis, I'm not sure how to respond.

There is no way anybody in their right mind would share this information with someone they don't know. They're basically admitting to stalking and I want nothing to do with them, but before I can say as much, they carry on speaking.

'I needed to know that the person who was working on this project with me was somebody who could fully appreciate the delicacy of the situations I wish to explore, but also show discretion and integrity. A talented writer can fully encapsulate the heart and the pain that only human nature can inflict, but they must be aware of these conflicts to display them fully to their readers. It may surprise you, but it was the flaws of those other men that drew me to them as writers, rather than their talents, but when I learned of what you have been through, Francesca, I knew you had experienced those emotions in a manner the others could not have dreamt of and we could use them to create a piece of art that will make the world stand up and notice us. And I believe that is what we both want. Is it not, Francesca? We want to make a piece of art the world takes notice of. Together, you and I can do that. I promise.'

My head is spinning, and the chill that filled my body only seconds ago has been replaced with a heat that burns in every cell. No wonder this person uses voice distortion and a pseudonym. They're crazy. A moderate stalker is the best-case scenario. The worst? Well, that doesn't bear thinking about. I clear my throat, still not sure what I'm going to say, when the conversation with Professor Jarvis resurfaces in my mind. He said that MI5 members and politicians require secrecy and anonymity for these projects. It makes sense that someone working in one of those roles would do their research on their writers. But to share that research, that's a power play. Manipulation, pure and simple.

'I don't think I'm the best person for this project after all,' I say. My voice trembles so much, I know they can hear my fear, but there's nothing I can do about it. 'I think you would be better off with someone more experienced.'

'Really? Well, that's a shame because you are already contractually obliged. Unless you have the means for legal fees? I'm not sure how much it costs to get a contract dissolved nowadays, but I'm sure you could look into it if that's the route you are determined to take.'

My throat is so tight it stings, and I have no idea how to respond, but in my silence, they speak again.

'I am sorry, Francesca. I should have realised the upset this would have caused you. Perhaps I should have kept my knowledge about your past a secret.' There's another pause and I'm sure they're waiting for me to speak, yet as I clear my throat again, they continue. 'I chose you because you are the right person. That was all I was trying to convey with my earlier comment. But from now on, I assure you, everything I mention will be directly related to the book. We can't say fairer than that, can we?'

I can't say anything at all. They've got me in a noose and they know that.

'I need you to send me profiles of the main characters, and any outlines of plots you have so far.' My voice is almost as stoic as the computer one I've been conversing with. 'We're done for tonight.'

'Of course. I will follow your expertise. And I'm sorry again, Francesca. We'll speak soon.'

A second later, the call is dead, and I drop my head into my hands.

What the hell have I got myself into?

20

I tell Heidi that I don't have time to stay for a glass of wine. Once again, I can tell she's disappointed, but when she sees my face, she understands there's no point in arguing.

'Is everything okay?' she says. 'You look upset.'

'I'm fine, I'm fine. I just need to get home.'

'Okay, well, we'll talk tomorrow. Maybe we can do a study session for Dr Ribero's poem. You know, critique each other?'

'Sounds good,' I say as I pick up my coat and hurry outside.

Heidi's flat is a forty-five-minute walk away, but that can be cut down to fifteen minutes if I take the Tube. That's exactly what I plan on doing until I approach the station.

I sense them before I see them. There's a tingle on the back of my neck, a nervousness that, for a second, I assume is just a hangover from the conversation with Dr B. I'm ready to dismiss it as such, but when I reach the cast-iron railings that mark the entrance to the Tube, something tells me to look over my shoulder. And when I do, I see them there. That same hoodie. Those same hunched shoulders.

There's a chance I'm just being paranoid. Lots of people wear hoodies. They're probably looking at their phone and that's why they're hovering. But there's still a niggling at the base of my skull.

We're not safe. Gloria's words ring out in my head. *He's... He's...*

No name. No insight. Just 'he'. That's what she kept saying. She couldn't get past that one word. Which 'he' was she referring to? Is it this person?

Before I realise what I'm doing, I turn on the ball of my foot and walk straight towards them.

'Hey!' I point my finger in their direction. 'Can I—'

The second I speak, they raise their hand, and I think they're going to reply, or maybe walk towards me, but before I can say more, they've spun around and are sprinting down the street. Any doubt I had has been erased. Someone has been following me, and I intend on knowing who and why.

With a speed I haven't mustered since school PE, I race after them.

'Wait! Wait! Who are you? Why are you following me? What do you want? Do you know Gloria?'

My words come out between breathless pants as I try to run as fast as I can, but my rucksack keeps slamming against my back, and I'm not a runner. I never have been. With every stride, this person is moving further and further away from me. I focus all my attention on the black hoodie. If I lose sight of them, it'll be game over. They take a left turn, and less than a minute later, I do the same. For a split second, I can see them there in the crowd, but then in a blink, they're gone. Still, I don't stop. I keep going. Keep running. There's no point. I know that. I'm slowing and there are just too many turns. Too many side streets they could have slipped down. Two minutes later, I'm standing at a crossroad. My head turns back and forth as I strain to see as far as I can, but deep down, I know there's no point. They've already gone.

21

I walk home, sticking to the busiest roads. So, at least I know I'm not paranoid now. Someone is definitely following me. Gloria? I dismiss the thought almost immediately. Unless she's changed dramatically over the past two years, she was never much of a runner. Besides, it's unlikely all of her curly black hair would fit under that hood without me spotting it. Then who?

He's...

I can't shake her words, or the fear in her voice when she spoke to me. But why am I so fixated on believing Gloria? It wasn't like anything else she said made sense. But I definitely didn't imagine the person following me. So who could it be?

One person springs immediately into my mind.

Dr B?

I consider the logistics. They didn't have their camera on, meaning they could've been anywhere, and with the use of the electronic voice, there wouldn't have been any microphone, meaning I wouldn't have heard any background noise. So, is Dr B the person she's worried about? Or rather, are they someone I need to be worried about?

Shit, what the hell is going on? Life was meant to be coming together. I was meant to be making something of myself. Now I'm just getting more and more paranoid.

As I approach our flat, I contemplate what to tell Duncan. He was so excited about looking for houses and so optimistic that today was going to be better. I know if I say that Dr B mentioned my parents, that will be it. He'll probably sell his guitars just to pay for the legal fees to get me out of this contract. And that won't help anybody. For now, at least, I think it's better just to stay quiet on the matter.

So, what about the fact I think I'm being stalked? Common sense tells me I should say something to Duncan about what just happened, but what if he puts it down to paranoia? It's not like I haven't got a history. When I was trying to convince the police that my father wasn't to blame for my mother's death, I turned up at the station almost every week for six months. Each time with a different suspect. A different name. Some of them I didn't even know. The woman who bullied my mum at a secretarial job five years beforehand. The man down the street who she would always yell at people for not picking up after their dogs. Not that we had a dog.

I mentioned some of this at the group counselling sessions where I met Duncan, and I saw his looks then. His pity. He felt so immensely sorry for me. Just like everyone in that room did. And just like everyone else, he thought I was lying to myself. That I was making up stories to alleviate some of the pain I felt. Even now, I've never mentioned how I still struggle to believe my father was guilty. What would be the point?

There's also the fact that I haven't even told him I spoke to Gloria yet. That wasn't deliberate; it's just that, with everything going on, there hasn't been time to shoehorn that conversation in too. Which is why, as I turn the key in the lock, I make a decision to say nothing. Not for now, not until I have a better idea of what's going on at least. And for that, I need to speak to Gloria. The question is, how do I get her to speak to me?

22

In an extremely rare occurrence, Duncan is out the door before me the next morning. An estate agent will do an apartment showing at 8 a.m. and he doesn't want to waste a scrap of time.

'It's the one with the balcony and it's going to be perfect, I can tell,' he tells me as he kisses me goodbye. Last night, I gave him an incredibly watered-down version of what happened the night before, telling him that Dr B was writing a thriller that involved lots of murder and they would be sending me character profiles to work with soon.

'See, I told you you were worrying about nothing,' he replied. After that, there was no way I could tell him about being followed or about Gloria. Not with it looking like it was coming out of nowhere.

'You've transferred the money to the joint account, right?' he says as he opens the front door. 'I want to be able to pay the deposit straight away. The last thing we want is someone beating us to it.'

'I'll do it now,' I say.

He gives me one more kiss before he leaves, and I head back

into the bedroom to open up my banking app. This is it. I know that. Spending this money means there's no way out of working for Dr B, but last night, Phil was smoking so much pot, I swear there were clouds coming in beneath the doorframe. Combined with the noise from his computer games, I've reached my limit. With a deep breath of cannabis-filled air, I hit send and transfer the money to the joint account. Then I get onto my second task of the day, persuading Gloria to meet with me.

> I think he's following me
>
> Tell me how I'm in danger
>
> Gloria I need your help

I send deliberately short messages that I know she'll be able to read on her locked screen, meaning even if she doesn't open my text, she won't be able to ignore me entirely. It's hard not to bombard her. There's certainly a part of me that wants to do that, but I have a plan in my mind. I'm going to walk to campus, go to my first lecture, then in the break before my next one, I'm going to sit outside, text her again, telling her I'm going to ring her. Hopefully, that will give her a chance to prepare, mentally anyway.

This version of my friend that I'm building up in my head is a polar opposite from the Gloria I lived with. That Gloria was as spontaneous as they come, but the version I spoke to two days ago, albeit briefly, sounded like a terrified animal, and I don't want to do anything to make her bolt.

My first lecture of the day is with Professor Jarvis, although there's no sign of him when I first walk into the hall. Instead, his PhD student is there setting up the laptop. I pretend not to see Heidi sitting in the front row, even when she waves to me. I slip into the back row, pretending to be fixated on my phone. Well, half-pretending. Duncan has already sent me three messages about the flat, telling me it's perfect and he's going to go for it if I'm all right with that. This is my last chance to back out, I understand that, but the thought of having somewhere other than Phil's pot-filled living room to relax in the evening is just too tempting.

Go for it, I say, before opening up my laptop and waiting for the lecture to begin.

I never normally struggle to concentrate, particularly during Professor Jarvis's lectures, but today is anything but normal. By the end of the hour, I've taken only about a third of the notes I normally do. I'm going to have to go back through the documents he places online and fill in all the information I've missed. My scholarship covers the cost of tuition, and without it, there's no way I'd be able to afford to stay here. But it's subject to review at the end of each year. The last thing I want is for the lecturers to decide they made a mistake. Particularly with the way I'm already struggling in the poetry class.

When we're finally dismissed, I bolt from the hall and head downstairs, where I take a seat on a bench. It's from here I start the second part of my plan to get Gloria to speak to me.

> I want to talk
>
> I'm going to ring you now
>
> Please pick up

I'm feeling absurdly nervous considering the person I'm hoping to talk to was supposed to be my best friend for years, but my pulse races as I hold my breath and hit the dial button.

This time, there's barely a single ring before she answers.

23

'We shouldn't be speaking,' Gloria starts immediately. 'It's not safe.'

'I know, I know it's not. Gloria—'

'I'm sorry, Frankie. I'm sorry, I didn't have a choice. I didn't...'

She descends into sobs, my heart burning in my chest.

'It's okay, it's okay,' I tell her. 'I know you didn't have a choice. You had to leave me, didn't you? I get that now. But I need you to tell me why. Who was it? Who is it that you're scared of? You have to tell me, Gloria, okay? This is so important, all right? I can help you. Help both of us. But you have to tell me, okay? You have to tell me now.'

'I can't... No. No.'

I instantly regret the manner in which I started the conversation. I'd already promised myself that I was going to take things slowly, listen to her and barely speak unless it felt necessary, but that's not worked out the way I planned. As I force myself to slow down, I hear her breath wheezing down the end of the line.

'Okay, it's okay, you're all right, Gloria, I promise. Look... I need to speak to you, okay? Properly. Not just like this. Can we meet? Can we meet somewhere safe, just you and me?'

There's a humming sound, and I'm pretty sure it's her shaking her head and refusing to speak. How the hell is this my Gloria? Where is the confident woman that was happy to live in a house where a murder had taken place, for crying out loud? I can't see her, but she sounds terrified of her own shadow. If I hadn't been so sure of her voice, I would think I was speaking to a stranger.

'Gloria, you trust me, don't you?' I speak firmly, using a confidence I'm not sure I feel.

'Yes,' she says between her sobs. 'I trust you.'

'Okay, and you trust that I will protect you—'

'You can't—'

'I will, I will. But I need you to meet with me, okay? I need you to meet with me, and we'll go somewhere safe, and it'll all be okay, all right?'

'He's not an angel, Frankie. He said he was an angel, but he wasn't.'

'It's all right, Gloria. I know. I know he's not an angel. You're okay. I know the truth.' She sounds like she needs serious help, and I'll get it for her. I will. Just as soon as I find out who's following me, and why Gloria suddenly left.

'There's a little café. I'm going to send you a pin, okay? A link to the map. I've got to go in a minute, I have a lecture, but I want you to meet me there at one o'clock for lunch, all right? Can you do that, Gloria?'

I fumble with my phone as I speak, trying to send the location without accidentally hanging up the call. After a moment, when I think I've managed it, I hear a ping on the end of her phone. 'That's it, you've got it, right? And you can meet me there?'

'Uh huh,' she says.

'What time? What time are you gonna meet me there,

Gloria?' It's like I'm talking to a freaking toddler, having to reinforce instructions dozens of times, but if that's what it takes, then that's what it takes.

'One. One o'clock.'

'That's right. I'll see you at one o'clock. Okay, Gloria. It'll be okay, I promise you.'

She sniffs, and I assume she's going to hang up, but instead, she speaks again.

'Don't make promises you can't keep,' she says. Then the line goes dead.

24

I go to stand, only to find my knees are uncharacteristically weak; that conversation took more out of me than I realised. My knees, my hands. There's a definite trembling stemming from my core, which has left my breath quivering. As I try to steady myself, I place my phone on the bench beside me and rest my hands on my knees.

'I'm starting to worry that you're not well.' I look up to find myself face to face with the same PhD student who spoke to me yesterday. The one who was setting up the laptop for Professor Jarvis's lecture. Once again, he has two cups of coffee in his hand. Is it demoralising or satisfying to be a general dogsbody for your idols? I can't be sure, but I've never noticed any of them looking particularly unhappy, so I guess it can't be all that bad. But is it something I would want to do? A week ago, I would have loved to have had that much access to Professor Jarvis and all his knowledge. Now, I'm not so sure.

'Right, sorry,' I say, realising he's looking at me like he's waiting for me to speak. 'No, I'm fine. Honestly, absolutely fine, just a lot going on at the moment.'

'Difficult call?' he says, nodding to the phone that I've placed by my side.

'Something like that.'

'Well, I better be getting inside; I'd hate for these to get cold.' He moves as if he's about to walk into the building, only to hesitate. 'All that stuff you've got going on at the moment, I don't suppose it's a boyfriend break-up, is it?'

I frown. 'No, why?'

'Well, I was just hoping that maybe, if you were single, we could get a coffee sometime.'

For a moment, silence follows his question, and then before I can stop myself, I throw back my head and laugh.

'I'm sorry,' I say hurriedly, realising how rude that must have come across. 'I wasn't laughing because I thought the idea was ridiculous. I mean, not because of you. I'm sure you're lovely. Really. But trust me, you don't want to date me. I'm not in a good place. And even if I was, my good place is a lot worse than most people's bad.' I pause, remembering one last fact. A fact I probably should have led with. 'Also, I have a boyfriend. A boyfriend I'm very happy with.'

This time, as he looks at me, a slight twist of a smile rises on his lips.

'Okay then, I'll take that as a no and leave you to it. But any more looking forlorn outside and I'll make it my personal mission to cheer you up. Or at least tell your boyfriend he needs to be doing a better job of making you smile.'

With that, he turns and leaves, and I bury my head in my hands. Life is just going from one point of ridiculousness to another.

25

The instant my lecture finishes, I'm out the door. The café is a ten-minute walk away, and it's not somewhere frequently populated by students. In fact, every time I've walked past it, it's been empty, which is why I picked it. The last thing I want is for Gloria to get spooked.

With every step, I try to prepare myself. Whatever has happened to Gloria in the last two years, it obviously hasn't been easy for her. Which means I need to tread carefully. If I don't, I doubt I'll get any answers.

The closer I get to the café, the greater my fear becomes. Until my parents' deaths, I'd lived an incredibly sheltered life. Sure, we moved a lot, but always to nice enough areas. Areas where we didn't have to worry about break-ins, or muggings, or people on the street because of drugs. Even after they died, and I stayed in the same rented house, my life was relatively easy in comparison to what many have to go through. Something tells me the same can't be said for Gloria.

When I reach the final turning, my heart rate is uncontrollable. There's a good chance Gloria is sitting outside, meaning that once I turn this corner, there's no going back. I'm going to have to talk to her. I'm going to have to hear her out.

I ready myself for whatever's about to come, draw in a deep breath, then make that turn, only to immediately draw to a stop.

The path in front of me is littered with police.

26

For a minute, I stand there and watch. There must be half a dozen police officers and dozens of people gathered around. Images rise in my mind. Memories, so similar to this moment, yet it wasn't on a busy street with passers-by stopping to observe the commotion; it was in a quiet cul-de-sac, with people coming out of their houses to nose and gossip. People who were still out there, an hour later when I strolled up to the house, not realising that my entire life had changed. Is this going to be another moment like that? Has my life changed yet again?

A wheezing sound alerts me to my breaths, which are becoming more and more shallow, while the sounds of the street have reached a near cacophony in my ears. As the intensity of the sensations rise, I scrunch my eyes closed and try to block them all out.

'You can feel your feet in your shoes. Your hand around your phone. The fabric of your top on your body.'

I'm whispering the words aloud, probably loud enough for someone passing by to hear, but I don't care. This is what I need to do. This is the most useful tool I got out of all those therapy sessions. The one grounding technique that really works for me. As I find more and more sensations to cling to, the noises begin to subside and differentiate. I can hear the chatter of people and the hum of traffic and the beat of my heart, all distinguishable from one another. My pulse begins to slow, and my mind comes back to the present. *I am safe. Duncan is safe. I am not in danger.* I repeat the mantras over and over in my mind until I know they're true and slowly I open my eyes.

The sight of the police causes another small spike in my adrenaline, but I do my best to suppress it as I edge towards them, trying to catch snippets of what's being said, but I can't. Someone's shouting, and it's getting louder and louder, making it hard to focus on anything else. When I get a little closer, I discover the source. A woman dressed in a café uniform is shouting at the police.

'You can't do this!' she yells. 'This is my business. My livelihood. She had nothing to do with me. It was nothing to do with me. She was a bloody druggy.'

'Ma'am, we need to go through all the proper procedures here. If you could just—'

'You're going to ruin me!' Her screams are perforated by gasping, wheezing sobs. By the looks of things, the police are shutting down her café, but why I can't tell. And if the café's closed, does that mean Gloria would just wait for me here, or would she go somewhere else? I check my phone, but there are no messages from her, so I move a little closer to the crowd. Finally, I catch wind of some of the other conversations.

'It was gross. She was vomiting as she was screaming. I'm going to have nightmares about that for months.'

'But do you think she really was poisoned? Who would have done that?'

'She was clearly a druggy.'

'She was wearing pretty nice clothes for a druggy.'

'Probably stole them.'

I've heard enough to know that I need more. Squeezing through several other baffled onlookers, I sidle up to the people talking.

'Sorry,' I say, speaking loud enough that they know I'm addressing them. 'You said a woman was poisoned here?'

'Well, a woman kicked off, saying she was poisoned.' The girl who speaks to me looks like a school student. Quite possibly truanting. She certainly doesn't look old enough to be at university yet, with her bright-pink hair and eyeliner so thickly applied, it looks like it's been drawn on with a marker. 'That's why she's kicking off.' She nods to the woman in the café uniform. 'The police want her to close shop until they know if there are any issues, but that's tight if you ask me. Anyone who'd seen the woman could tell she was crazy. Drugged up to the eyeballs.'

'Where is she now?' I ask, looking around. There's no one yelling about being poisoned any more. The only yelling is coming from the café owner, who's still protesting about being shut down.

'They took her away in an ambulance. She started doing this whole convulsing thing. You know, like people do when they're overdosing.'

'So you think she was poisoned?'

'By herself, maybe.'

The second girl lets out a light chuckle, and a wave of anger ripples through me. They're young. They have no idea how quickly life can change. I hope for their sake they don't find out.

Clearly done with our conversation, they shift their bodies so they're once again facing away from me, but I still have one other question I need to ask. One I'm sure I have the answer to already.

'Sorry,' I say, then repeat myself, tapping her shoulder when she doesn't immediately turn around. 'Sorry, but what did the woman look like? The one who was saying she was poisoned?'

The girl rolls her eyes as if I've just asked her the most uninteresting question in the world, and she reinforces this idea with a slight sigh, before she speaks.

'Oldish. Your age, I guess. Dark, curly hair, though mostly that was filled with vomit. And cute pink sunglasses. Retro style. I was thinking I might get a pair like that myself.'

I step back, no longer interested in anything the girls are saying. I've found out what I needed to know for sure. The woman they're talking about is Gloria. The druggy who thought they'd been poisoned is my old best friend, who wanted to warn me I was in danger. A churning dread fills the pit of my stomach. The question is, what do I do now?

27

For close to twenty minutes, I try to get some information out of the police. Further confirmation of what I know is true.

'Do you have a name for the girl taken off in an ambulance?' I ask every police officer I see.

I try to explain that I was meeting a friend who isn't here, and I'm worried that it could have been her. A couple let me get as far as giving my explanation. Others just tell me I need to get out of the way and stop wasting police time. One ignores me entirely, as if I'm invisible.

I've tried calling Gloria too. I've sent half a dozen messages which all remain unread. Of course, that doesn't mean she's in hospital. She might just have gone back to ignoring me.

It doesn't take long before the owner relents and shuts up the café, although she's still not stopped yelling; instead, she's saying that she's going to sue the police for loss of earnings. I'm not sure that's something she can do, but I admire her for not giving up.

After the police have spoken to everyone they want to, the crowd disperses. More than one officer tells me the show's over and it's time to go home, and I know they're right, I won't get any more information standing around here, but I can't do nothing, can I? I need someone to help me, and there's only one person in the world who can do that.

I find Duncan packing up our belongings in the bedroom.

'Hey, what are you doing here?' he says. 'Did you not read my message?'

'Message? What? Sorry, no. What did you say?'

'We've got the keys.' He lifts a heavy keyring from his pocket. 'I thought you'd want to meet me there. I was going to move everything across. The band was going to help. You know, try to make it as homely as possible, but I guess now you're here, you can help.'

'How did you get them so fast? I thought it would take a couple of days to sort things. Check finances, that type of stuff.'

His grin widens. 'It should have done, but the landlord turned up while we were looking at the place, and I started telling her how I was so excited, and it would really help my girlfriend to have a quiet place to work on her novel. I mean, I laid it on pretty thick and everything, but it obviously worked. She said I could have the keys as soon as they got the deposit. Which I sent to them then and there. And voila.' He jangles the keys and I know I should look pleased about this, but I'm having a hard time even focusing on what he's saying.

'Right, right,' I say, only to shake my head. 'Actually, we need to stop packing.'

'What?'

'I need to tell you something.'

He places his T-shirts down on the bed.

'Frankie, what is it? You haven't changed your mind, have you? You don't want to get that place? I knew I should have checked. I mean, I don't know if I can—'

'That's not it, that's not it, it's... it's about Gloria.'

'Gloria?' His face hardens. 'What about her?'

'I spoke to her.'

'What?'

'I spoke to her and… I think something's happened to her. I'm worried, Duncan. I'm really, really worried.'

28

By the time I've finished telling him everything that's happened, his jaw is so tightly clenched, I can see the muscles twitching.

'It's her,' he says. 'Surely you can tell that. She has to be the one that was following you. It makes sense. Why else would she suddenly start speaking to you again now?'

'But it didn't look like her, it didn't. And this stuff with Dr B…'

'What stuff with Dr B?'

I steel myself against however he's going to respond, but I've already told him most of the story; I might as well let him know the rest.

'He knows about my parents. He mentioned he was writing a murder-suicide and wanted to check I would be okay with it because of my past.'

Duncan's face turns from pale to near purple.

'He said what? Jesus, Frankie, you need out of this. You need out of this now.'

'There's no way out of it, Duncan. I've already spoken to Professor Jarvis. The lawyers, the cost… It's impossible. I just have to get through it.'

He presses his lips so tightly together, I can almost hear his brain whirring.

'You've never heard this Dr B's voice, have you?'

'You know I haven't; it's all done through the computer.'

'So there's a good chance it could be a woman? It could be Gloria?'

'Gloria?' I say, raising my eyebrows. 'No.' I shake my head. 'This type of thing costs money. Serious money. She wouldn't have that. Besides, did you not listen to what I said about the ambulance? About the police? I'm sure it was her. Please, Duncan. I know you can't forgive her, but she didn't play games like this before. She didn't. Apart from leaving. And I think she wanted to tell me the reason she did that today. She was scared, Duncan. I think it's drugs, but it could be something else too. Please, can you help me do this? I need to ring the hospital to see if she was the person taken away in an ambulance.'

Once again, his lips disappear into a thin line, then he lets out a slight sigh before he plants a kiss on the top of my head.

'Of course I will,' he says. 'Let's make a list of places to ring. But trust me, you're not going to find her. I'd bet our new flat on it.'

29

My plan was to ring the closest hospital to the café, having assumed the ambulance would go straight there, but Duncan informs me it's not always as straightforward as going on distance.

'When my grandad had a heart attack, they took him to a hospital that was twenty miles further away than the closest one because they knew they could place a stent in his heart immediately. If they think they know what's wrong with her, and there's a specialist place within a reasonable distance, then they might go to that hospital instead.'

'Are there specialist places for people having an overdose?'

'You think she was on drugs?'

'I don't know. She didn't sound right to me, but I only spoke to her briefly. But the people at the café, the people who saw her, they all said she sounded like she was. It might be worth considering, right? Is there somewhere else they would have taken her if that was the case?'

He shakes his head. 'Not that I know of. I guess there are

rehab centres, but if she was in that bad of a state, I'm sure she'd have to go to a hospital first.'

I nod; it makes sense.

'Okay, let's start with the hospitals, then move to the rehab centres after that.'

Three hours. That's how long Duncan and I are on the phone, calling different hospitals and health centres and even doctor's surgeries, asking if a Gloria Coles had been brought in at any point that day. I give them as much information as I can. She would have been brought in by an ambulance from a café on Highworth Street around eleven-ish. She's twenty-nine, I tell them, with curly hair just above her shoulders. I say how it was a suspected drug overdose, though I also add that she was mentioning poisoning at the time the ambulance was called. I give them her date of birth and even go as far as telling them she was wearing pink sunglasses. Duncan starts with the basics. Name, age and time she'd have been brought in, but by the time he's on his sixth call, he can repeat what I say almost word for word.

It's not the speaking that takes time, though; it's the waiting between the talking. People put us on hold while they check with A&E, or intensive care, or just on the hospital database. And at the end of every conversation, we are told exactly the same thing.

'No one of that name has come into our hospital today.'

And each time I receive the news with a mixture of disappointment and relief.

'I think we need to call it a day,' Duncan says as he looks at his watch. 'On the plus side, this is good news, isn't it? If she's not in hospital, it means it wasn't her. She's still okay.'

'She wasn't okay, Duncan. She really wasn't.'

He purses his lips and there's something about his expression that I can't read. That's not usual for us. We normally know exactly what the other one is thinking.

'What? Whatever it is, just spit it out.'

He chews the moment over for a second before he moves across the room and sits next to me on the bed.

'I know you said that Gloria didn't play games before she left, but that's not entirely true. She played lots. You just didn't see them.'

'What do you mean? What kind of games? What are you talking about?' It's my time to come in with the repetitive questions, though Duncan is frustratingly slow to answer. Instead, he picks at his nail.

'I know you thought the world of her, but I have to be honest. I was relieved when she was out of your life.'

'What?' My jaw drops so fast, I feel the muscles click. 'You and her got on well?'

'We got on well because I didn't have any choice in the matter. It was either I shared you with her or she pushed me out. She threatened me. Said she was going to tell you I came onto her. That I did worse than that.'

'What? Why the hell didn't you say anything to me?'

'I don't know. She always packaged it up like it was a joke. Not to mention the number of times she told me that if I made you choose between me and her, then you'd always choose her. And I wasn't going to do that. Not after everything you'd already lost. I just think you should know. She wasn't quite as great as she made out. I think you were lucky she got out of your life when she did.'

I feel my head shaking, though I'm not sure if it's a deliberate act or not.

'Wow, well, today has been full of surprises, that's for sure.' I pull in a lungful of air, which I let out in a huff. 'She was really going to do that. Say you... you came onto her.'

'We'd only been together a couple of months when she said that, and she didn't do it again, but it stuck with me. That unease. I never trusted her after that. I'm sorry, I know you thought a lot of her, and I get she was amazing at helping you to cope with… with your parents' passing. But I told you the truth when she left, remember? I told you I thought she preyed on you. That she picked you to befriend because she thought she could somehow fix you. Not that I think you need fixing, you know that, right? You know I love you more than anything, and I'd never make anything like this up. I'd never make up something to hurt you, you know that, don't you?'

'Of course I do.'

He smiles, but it's weaker than I'd expect.

'Well, good, because we've got a flat to move into together. And tonight, if you're still up for it?'

30

We don't have a proper contract with Phil. When we moved in, he said, quite succinctly, 'Don't screw me over and I won't screw you over,' and considering he's the reason we haven't slept properly in nearly a year and a half, I don't feel even an ounce of guilt at leaving him to find someone else to fill our room. Who knows, he might have a dozen gaming friends who've just been waiting for us to move out and he's been too polite to tell us he wants us to leave. I doubt it, but it's possible.

With most of the evening gone ringing around looking for Gloria, we focus our attention on packing our lives into boxes. I'm not surprised by how little time it takes. We're not materialistic people and the only items I own a vast quantity of are books, and most of those are still in boxes from when I finally moved out of my parents' rental house. Still, it's not until ten-thirty that we are standing outside the door to our new apartment.

'Okay,' Duncan says, stopping at the bottom of the stairs. 'I probably should have told you this before, but I gave Tommy and the band a key to the place.'

'What? You're planning on practising here?'

I love Duncan, but that was never in our agreement. I socialise with the band occasionally, but only on my terms. I can't imagine having my house constantly filled with people and me not being able to do anything about it. The thought makes me feel sick.

'No, we're not going to be using this place to practice. Don't worry, you'll see. Now, close your eyes. Actually, let's wait till you get to the top of the stairs. You can close your eyes then.'

He leads me up to the top floor by hand, so excited, he's practically bouncing up and down.

'Bear in mind, if you don't like it, this is not my fault. Are you ready for this?'

'Maybe?' I say.

A moment later, he clicks open the front door to our flat. My jaw drops.

'You did all this today?' I had been expecting to walk into an empty flat with boxes all over the floor, but this looks like a home. A minimalist one, but still a home.

'Well, the guys did most of it,' Duncan says. 'And in case you hate it, you should know that nothing is permanent. And don't worry about the pictures on the wall; they're just tacked on, although the landlord said she was okay with the odd nail here and there. I already put one just there for your keys. I know you like a place to hang them, but I didn't want to do anything until you decided if you liked it.'

Even at this time of night, there's so much light. Light and space. No longer are we going to be confined to a tiny, dark bedroom. This is the type of space where you could really entertain and have people over. If that was something I did.

Then there's the furniture. There's not a lot, but it's better than none. There's a desk and chair, along with two other turquoise tub chairs that I've never seen before.

'Where did you get all this?' I ask. 'I thought the place was unfurnished.'

'Someone was giving them away online. There's also a blowup mattress in the bedroom, which Tommy lent me. We'll have to give it back, but I'm sure I can find a cheap bed in the next couple of days.' He pauses, and a look of concern flashes on his face as he takes my hand. 'So, is it okay? Are you happy?'

'Are you serious? This is better than I could have dreamt.'

His smile goes so high, his eyes almost disappear.

'Well, I've got at least twenty minutes before I have to leave. What do you say we check out the sturdiness of the blowup bed?'

The last couple of days have been one thing after another, and I'd assumed that all I'd want to do was curl up in bed and sleep. But as I look at Duncan, who's looking at me that way, I'm suddenly not quite so sleepy.

'That sounds good,' I tell him.

31

It's not until the next morning that I fully explore the apartment. Not that there's that much to explore. It's two beds with an open-plan living area. Still, I open every drawer and cupboard.

Our bedroom looks out over the front of the building, and in the hope of glimpsing one of our neighbours, I lose at least ten minutes staring out of the window. When someone finally does walk in, it's not one person – it's three: a couple with a pushchair.

The sight brings a sense of comfort. After all, if they find it quiet and safe enough to raise a child, then that's got to be a good sign.

Feeling even more confident that Duncan's picked us a good place, I move through to the front of the house and open the double doors onto the balcony. I'm sure there are thousands of balconies in the city with better views than this one, but at this moment, I can't believe that. There's space and light – something my body has been craving for months now, and while I know the air isn't any fresher up here – it's a few floors, not a mountain climb – I swear it feels like it is. With my hands on the rail, I close my eyes and take a deep inhale. When I open them again, I glance downwards and spot a small bouquet of flowers tucked away in the corner.

'Duncan, you old romantic,' I say. I suspect he meant to give them to me last night but put them out here while he was sorting things and forgot about them. As such, I don't feel any guilt in picking them up. There's a small card perched on top between some of the larger blooms. Flowers aren't Duncan's normal style of gesture, but sweet little notes are. Already anticipating the words I'll find inside, I open the envelope and read the card.

Frankie, may this home be happier than your last ones.

It's not the romantic note I was hoping for, and the rushed scrawl barely looks like Duncan's writing, but maybe I was expecting too much. After all, he found the place, moved us in here, got the boys to help decorate it. All while working. It's not like he's had a lot of free time. Maybe there's a story behind it? Maybe he was going to comment about Phil and the pot and his video games. That would make sense. Regardless of the meaning, I need to thank him.

Taking the flowers with me, I head back into the apartment and into the bedroom, where Duncan is still dozing away.

'I found your flowers,' I say, sitting on the corner of the bed. The air mattress dips, causing him to roll over towards me.

'Hey, you.' He yawns and blinks a couple of times before opening his eyes. 'What's up?'

'I just wanted to say thank you for the flowers. They're beautiful.'

'What flowers?' He's still rubbing his eyes as he pushes himself up to sitting.

'The ones you were supposed to give me yesterday. The ones you left on the balcony?'

'I didn't leave any flowers on the balcony, Frankie. I meant to get you some, though. I wanted to put a bunch on the table for when you came home, but I ran out of time.'

The warmth is draining from my body. Without another word, I stand up and get the flowers from where I had placed them in the kitchen.

'Nope,' Duncan says as soon as I reappear with the bouquet in my hands. 'I have never seen them before.'

My entire body feels icy cold.

'Then who the hell put them there?' I say.

32

'I'm sure it was one of the boys,' Duncan says as he sees the panic cross my face. 'I mentioned I wanted to get you some. They probably just picked some out for me.'

'And what about the weird note?' I say. Only a few minutes ago, I'd looked at the flowers with a sense of warmth. Now they make me feel nauseous. 'Who would write that?'

'It's really not that weird. We were miserable in the last place. Everyone knows that.'

'Then why did they just address them to me, and why didn't they put their name on the note?'

I don't understand why Duncan isn't freaking out about this. There's something in our home that's addressed to me and we don't know how it got there.

'Frankie, you don't need to worry, I will talk to the boys. I promise, there is some incredibly rational explanation for this. I promise you.' He takes my hand and locks his eyes on mine. 'You trust me, right?'

It feels like a trick question in that he knows there's only one answer I can give. 'Of course I do,' I say, though I preceded my words with a sigh, which he ignores.

'Okay, then trust me when I say there is nothing to worry about. I will find out where they came from. Now, I've got to leave in half an hour so do you want to spend that time worrying about nothing, or do you want to see if you can fit two people in the shower?'

I know he's trying to distract me, but Duncan generally has a good read on things. He said it was going to be tough-going living with Phil before we moved in there, and he wasn't wrong about that. If he thinks it's from one of the boys then I should probably believe him. After all, flowers and a note aren't exactly threatening behaviour.

'The shower's enormous,' I say finally. 'There's definitely room for the two of us.'

'How are we going to know for sure if we don't try?'

Duncan's eyes glint with mischief and for the first time since discovering the flowers weren't from him, I feel a smile lift on my lips.

'Maybe I could do with a quick shower,' I say.

'Now that sounds like an idea. Although maybe less of the quick.' He grins.

33

'I'm going to be late back tonight,' Duncan says when we're out of the shower, dried and dressed. 'It's a wedding gig. Oh, and I forgot to say, there's a bottle of Prosecco in the fridge from Tommy and the others, but you're not allowed to open it until I get back, okay? Unless you're desperate, in which case go for it.'

The fact the boys brought Prosecco makes it feel even more likely that the flowers were from them too.

'I'm sure I can hold off,' I tell him, pressing my body against his as I kiss his lips. Freedom to be like this, freedom to be together without worrying we're infringing on someone else's space, isn't something we've had much of, and I can already see how much better life is going to be here.

'When's your next ghost-writing session?' he says when we break apart.

The thought of Dr B immediately dampens my mood.

'I don't know. I'm waiting for them to send the character profiles through.'

'Well, I'm gigging all weekend, but I've nothing on Monday

other than a couple of private lessons during the day, so maybe see if you can avoid that night.'

'I will try my hardest,' I tell him, though as I move to kiss him again, he catches sight of the time on my phone.

'Crap, I need to get going,' he says. 'I've got a music lesson to teach. Love you.'

'Love you too.'

After Duncan leaves, I can't help but try Gloria's number, but each time, the call goes straight through to answerphone. Part of me wants to drop the issue and forget about her the way Duncan wishes I would, but a large part is aware that I still have a chunk of time before I have to leave for my lecture.

Not wanting to waste any of it, I drop down onto the bed and begin calling the list of numbers of my most recent dials. They are all the same hospitals and clinics we rang immediately after Gloria didn't show at the café, and I know they all told me she hadn't been admitted to them, but I need to check for updates. Perhaps someone missed something. Or it was a new person working who didn't understand the systems properly. There has to be a reason I can't get hold of her.

I know Duncan would think I'm ridiculous. He thinks this is her MO. But there's a difference between this and when she went last time. Sure, when she left me before, it came out of the blue, but she was in a much better headspace. She could talk straight, for starters. The Gloria I spoke to this time needed help, I'm sure of it.

Three phone calls in and I'm feeling despondent.

'Where the hell are you, Gloria?' I let the words out as a near scream, before releasing the rest of the air in my lungs as a long sigh.

Once again though, nobody by her name has been in the hospitals within the last week. I'm not going to give up, though.

Maybe I'll start putting flyers out. Enough missing-people charities do them, so they must have some impact.

If she would just answer one of my texts or calls, then I would let her be, but it's niggling away at me, and I won't be able to drop it until I know she's okay. It's not even about whether she wants me in her life any more. I just need to know she's still alive.

Knowing that I've done as much as I can for now, I grab my things and head out. I spent more time on the phone than I'd planned, which means walking fast to make sure I'm not late, yet as I approach the English building, I'm slowed by a group of people gathered on the pathway.

'Do you know her? Do you know where I can find her?'

It's an older man who's speaking, and several people respond, though none of them seem to be answering his question.

'Are you coming back to lecture again?'

'Would you be able to sign my copy of *Webs and Weavers*?'

'Can I just ask you about the theme in—'

'Francesca Crawford!' He raises his voice to a near shout. 'Can anybody tell me where I will find a student here by the name of Francesca Crawford?'

I step forward, only for my body to freeze part way through the motion. The man speaking is none other than Rupert Fitzherbert. Noted author and former lecturer. His hair is dishevelled and eyes red-rimmed as they lock onto mine.

'Francesca Crawford,' he says.

My chin involuntarily dips into a nod.

'Tell me you're joking,' he says, looking straight at me. 'Tell me that arsehole didn't just give you my payout?'

34

I feel my mouth open and my tongue move up and down inside it, as if it's going to say something, but no words actually come out.

Several people are looking at us.

'So, is it true?' Rupert says. 'Did that arsehole give the job to you?'

There are so many ways I want to reply to his question, but there's only one answer I can actually give.

'Yes,' I say.

'Fucking hell.' He throws his hands up in the air as he looks at the sky. 'This is a fucking joke. Seriously, you? Why? You're a nothing. You have no experience. You're a student, for crying out loud, probably living off all your student loans. This project is worth over fifty grand. What the hell do you need that kind of money for?'

Dr B's words about how Rupert has a gambling problem ring in my mind. Had I not believed they were telling the truth then, I do now.

'I don't know what you want me to say,' I said. 'I did an interview, and they chose me.'

Rupert scoffs. 'What I want you to do is give me that job. Quit and give it to me. It's mine. One more interview; that's all he said I had to do. One more interview and then it was mine. I'd already had four, for crying out loud. And then you come along and steal it out from under me.'

It's more than just one or two people looking at us now. There are probably close to a dozen, and there is very little I hate more than so many pairs of eyes on me. It's something I had to deal with so much in the past.

But it doesn't make me back down. I've already gone through enough shit with this Dr B character to take even more from someone I barely know. I lower my voice and lock my eyes on his as I speak.

'I get that you're upset about this,' I say. 'But you're getting cross with the wrong person here. I didn't even want the job. I'd rather you took it.'

He's still scoffing and grunting as he continues to shake his head. 'Oh, how very inconvenient for you. I'm sure you'd make that very straightforward. Let me guess, you'd just want paying out of the contract? Of course you would.'

There are too many people looking at us now. I need this conversation to end. It's one thing dealing with Dr B, who's paying me, but this? I don't have to deal with this. As renowned as Rupert Fitzherbert is, he's nothing to me.

'I might not know anything about Dr B's thinking in hiring me,' I say truthfully. 'But from the way you're acting here now, I can't help thinking that maybe it was your lack of professionalism that stopped you from getting the job in the first place?'

'How dare you, you little shit. I was published while you were still in fucking—'

'Rupert?' My head spins to find Professor Jarvis standing there, looking at the pair of us, his brow crinkled in confusion. 'What are you doing here? What's going on?'

'Did you do this?' Rupert said. 'Is this your doing? You know, I knew you were conniving. I knew that, but to stab me in the back, you fu—'

'Rupert, I think I know what this is about, but this isn't the place to have this conversation. I think we should move into my office, please.' Rupert opens his mouth to object, but Professor Jarvis cuts across him before he can say anything else. 'Now, or I will be forced to call security.'

This time, he moves.

35

I initially thought that the offer to move into Professor Jarvis's office was solely for Rupert, but as the lecturer gestures for Rupert to go inside, his eyes meet mine, and he offers me a slight dip of his chin. Instinctively, I look at the time on my phone. I have a lecture starting in ten minutes. I just have to hope that this doesn't take long, or Professor Jarvis can explain the situation so my attendance doesn't drop.

When we reach his office, the PhD student is standing outside with a stack of books in his arms, obviously wanting to talk.

'This'll have to wait, Will,' Professor Jarvis says as he opens his door and lets us in.

'Okay, I'll come back later,' the PhD student says. 'How about in half an hour?'

Professor Jarvis doesn't reply. Instead, he just closes the door with the student on the other side of it, then wordlessly moves around the desk to take a seat. He holds seminars in this room, so there are also half a dozen other seats. I choose the one closest to the door, hoping that Rupert will pick one as far away from me as possible.

'So, I assume this is about the ghost-writing project,' Professor Jarvis starts.

'You knew she'd got it?'

'I did; she told me earlier in the week. And she has a name, by the way. It's Francesca.'

Rupert snorts. 'It's ridiculous. You know it is. I mean, it doesn't happen like that. You work your way up a business. You don't get handed the biggest client on the book on the first day.'

'I didn't get handed it on a plate,' I say. 'I interviewed for it and I got the job.' My stomach twists a little. I could add that I got offered it because my dad was a murderer, but I don't think that would enamour Rupert to me any further, though I do still have another point to make. One that I'm probably not going to get a chance to voice again. 'Would you have accosted me outside my university if I was a man? Because I don't think you would have done. I don't think this is just about me being a new writer. It's about me being a young, new, female writer. If I were a man, I'd be "up-and-coming". I have some gusto about me. Potential. Instead of being a conniving bitch who is usurping your place.'

'I'm pretty sure I was spot on with my conniving bitch assessment—'

'Enough!' Professor Jarvis slams his hand against a tabletop. 'Rupert, this is ridiculous. You know that the client alone is the one who decides who gets these positions.'

'But you put her name forward. Why? You never do that. Never. What's so special about her?'

I expect Professor Jarvis to answer straight away that he read a piece of my work and that he knew from my writing that I was capable. But his Adam's apple bobs up and down and there's a heartbeat's delay before he replies.

'I put Francesca's name forward because she is an exceptional writer,' he says, although his eyes skirt past me as he says this. And I'm not the only one who notices.

'Bullshit,' Rupert says.

'It's the truth.' This time, Professor Jarvis is more convincing. 'I put her name forward, but that's all I did. I don't have the power to do more than that, and you know it. The client obviously chose her for a reason, and that's not up to you or me to question. You know that. You also know, or at least I hope you know, that coming onto a university campus and verbally threatening a student is not a great look. Especially when it's a university that you have already been dismissed from.'

'What are you saying?' Rupert's voice is nothing more than a low growl, although Professor Jarvis remains completely unperturbed. I, on the other hand, feel myself shrink inwards.

'You heard me. If you set foot in here again, I will have the campus security escort you off-site and it will be up to Miss Crawford whether she takes matters further. Do you understand?'

Rupert's mouth is so far open, he could catch flies, and his eyes move between me and Professor Jarvis when he lets out, 'You're fucking her, aren't you?'

'Excuse me?'

'You're fucking her. That's why you did this. Jesus fucking Christ.'

He moves as if he's going to stand, but before he gets there, Professor Jarvis has whipped around from his desk and is standing over the top of him, blocking him from getting up.

'You need to watch your mouth,' he snarls. 'You're getting sloppy, Rupert. Do you want to know why you didn't get that job? It's because you're lazy. You think you should be handed things on a plate when you haven't written a novel of your own creation for the last seven years. Get some new ideas. Get a new attitude, and then you might get some bloody work.'

Rupert's mouth continues to hang open, but he doesn't say anything. Instead, he swallows visibly. Without so much as a glance in my direction, Professor Jarvis steps back to give him room to stand up.

'Now get out of my office and stop judging people by your own vile standards,' he says.

36

Rupert doesn't need telling twice. A moment later, he's on his feet, marching out of the office. He slams the door so hard that several books fall off the shelves, but rather than picking them up, Professor Jarvis drops back into his seat and lets out a sigh.

'I'm so sorry. Rupert has some issues. However that came across, it wasn't personal, I can assure you.'

'I know,' I reply, thinking about Dr B's words and how Rupert has a gambling problem.

'The publishing world, it's a funny old place. As much as some of us old dogs don't like to hear it, you have to evolve to stay relevant. It's the reason I maintain this position at the school, and will do so however well my writing career is going. I think it's important that I stay in the loop with younger writers. Keep an ear to the ground, so to speak. Writers like Rupert, who live locked away in their little corner, assume they're constantly relevant to the world, despite making no effort to be part of it. I think recently he's started to realise that, and it's having an impact.'

A silence falls between us, a contemplative one, and I suspect he is thinking about far more than just Rupert or me. It feels like I need to excuse myself.

'Well, thank you, Professor Jarvis—'

'Ivor, please. Call me Ivor.'

'Sorry, yes. Ivor. I should get going.' I move to stand before he is talking to me again.

'The job, though, everything else with it is going okay?'

My pulse skips to a notch higher as I think about the way Dr B casually mentioned my parents and how, whenever I think about our next meeting, my stomach knots with a sense of fear, causing all the hairs to bristle on the back of my neck. But I'm tied to it, though that's not the only reason I don't want to say anything. Professor Jarvis is the person who put me forward and introduced me to the ghost-writing business. The last thing I want is to come across as incapable of doing a task that he recommended me for.

I force my cheeks to rise into a smile.

'Everything's going just fine,' I lie.

37

Dr B has impeccable timing, I'll give them that. Only two minutes after I leave Dr Jarvis's office, I get an email through asking if tonight would work for a meeting, although there's no sign of the character profiles they were going to give me.

I don't want to meet with them in the slightest, but I can't say no. Prolonging meetings will just prolong how long I have them in my life. Besides, I have questions I want to ask him, and they're not to do with the novel.

Determined to put Rupert Fitzherbert and his outburst behind me, I head to my first lecture despite being ten minutes late. I then spend the remainder of the morning looking over my poem for Dr Ribero before I send it off. At least that's one thing I've ticked off my list of things to do. Fingers crossed it will be a better grade than the previous one.

When I finish my last lecture of the day, I head to the library, ready to sort out my notes and get on with some reading, the way I've done almost every weekday for the last year and a half. Only when I go to sit down, I remember I actually have a quiet place I can work now. A home I actually want to go to and a boyfriend who is probably waiting for me. Unfortunately, it doesn't look like we're going to get much time together tonight.

'I can find another bassist to sub in for me if you want me to stay with you for your meeting,' Duncan says as he prepares to leave only an hour after I've got in. 'I don't mind being with you.'

'We need the money,' I remind him. 'Rent on this place is a lot more than at Phil's, remember?'

I haven't told him about Rupert yet. I'd planned on doing so, but then when I got home, he'd made me dinner, found another armchair which he'd placed facing the window so I could enjoy the view and even scored a double bed, although it is currently lying flat in a pile of wooden slats, waiting for us to have the time to put it together. After all that, the last thing I wanted to do was cause him even more stress.

'Have you thought any more about what I said? About how it could be Gloria you're speaking to behind that computer voice.'

I hadn't. Not seriously, anyway. I don't see what Gloria would have to gain from speaking to me like that. She knows everything about me. And if she wanted to talk, she could just pick up the phone and ring me. Assuming she wasn't carted away from a café in an ambulance. Gloria is one riddle, Dr B another, but I don't think they're linked.

'I don't think it's her,' I say. 'I doubt she has enough money for the initial payment, let alone the rest of it.'

Duncan doesn't respond. It's unusual for him to show this level of nervousness, so I try even harder to hide my own apprehension.

'It'll be fine,' I say, looping my arms around his waist so I can pull him in closer to me. 'It's a conversation, that's all. And I've already decided I'm going to record what they say.'

Duncan's frown lines deepen. 'You know it says in your contract you're not meant to do that, right?'

'Well, people leave the recorder on their phone on by accident all the time. And it's not like anyone will find out. It's just for you and me. That's all.'

He purses his lips before he speaks. 'Whatever you think is best,' he says. 'And we're not playing tonight until nine-thirty, so if you change your mind and want me here, I can come back.'

'And let the band down?'

'Yes, absolutely. If that's what you need.'

I believe him. I know he would 100 per cent ditch whatever he was doing, no matter how important it was, if he thought I needed him. But I have no intention of doing that.

'I love you,' I tell him. 'And I'll be fine.'

'I'll come straight home tonight. Just text me, okay? Keep me in the loop. I want to know if they say anything else strange, immediately. You get it? I don't want you holding on to these things yourself. Not even overnight. That's not how we work. We're a team.'

A squirm of guilt twists in my belly as I think about all the things I've recently kept from him, even though I'm only doing it for his own good. Would he do the same? I wonder. Keep things from me, if he thought I was better off not knowing? It seems unlikely. What could he possibly tell me that would be worse than I've already been through?

'Of course,' I say, holding his gaze the best I can. 'A team.'

38

I open the call bang on nine, and Dr B is there straight away.

'I'm sorry I didn't get to send the character profiles through. I wanted to discuss them with you a little first,' the electronic voice says. Strangely, I've become so accustomed to it, I barely hear its monotony any more. Or perhaps I'm just more focused on what I want to say than what they're saying.

'We'll get to that,' I reply. 'First, though, I need to know something. Did you tell Rupert you were going to offer him the job?'

'Rupert?'

It may still be the same digital voice, but I know they're feigning ignorance. They know exactly who I'm talking about.

'Rupert Fitzherbert, remember? You mentioned him last session. You said he had a gambling problem. Did you tell him you were going to offer him this job?'

A pause follows. I've gotten used to those now, and I expect this one, coming from their end, will last longer than normal. It spreads tangibly, possibly because they have a lot to type. I don't know. Finally, a response buzzes through.

'Not exactly,' they respond. 'I told him that if he had another interview, I would offer him the job. Obviously, I did not request him for any further interviews. Why? Has he been pestering you?'

'Not exactly.'

This time, the reply comes immediately. 'What does that mean? I take it he's been in contact with you?'

Dr B may have the advantage of a black screen and digitised voice to help hide their emotions, but I don't have that luxury and I know I'm a terrible liar, and as such, I make the split-second decision that it's probably easier just to give them a half-truth. 'He was upset,' I say. 'I don't believe he was informed that he hadn't got the position, or that I had.'

Once again, there's only a slight gap between me finishing and Dr B's voice coming through.

'I don't understand why he'd be upset about that. I'm sure this isn't the first position he's applied for that he's not got. He knows how this works, but by all means, let me know if he harasses you again, and I will take it up with higher authorities.'

There's something about the way they used the words 'pestering' and 'harassing' that unnerves me. Do they assume that's what he did because it's something they would do?

'I can assure you the issue was dealt with,' I tell them. 'I just wanted to know from your point of view, that's all.'

'From my point of view, Rupert Fitzherbert is an arrogant arse who has sailed through life based on vaguely good looks and a minimal scraping of charisma, and now that both are failing him, he is flailing.'

It's a damn harsh character assessment – closer to a character annihilation – and feels incredibly personal for someone they were merely going to employ for a job. Especially considering that only two minutes ago, they'd pretended not to remember who Rupert was. Still, I do feel that Rupert's assumption that the job was his was exactly that: an assumption.

'Now, onto my novel. I've got lots I want you to get researching.'

39

Dr B has a specific way for me to work laid out in their mind. We will meet three times a week, adding a weekend session in only if they deem it necessary, and I will need to send them the work at a rate of ten thousand words a week, with a possible increase when we are halfway. It's a hefty start but hopefully, working this way will mean the project will be completed quickly. That means the next payday will come quicker and when it's all done, I'll not only have time to write, but money too. And, perhaps most importantly, Dr B will be out of my life for good.

By the end of the first two full sessions, I am more used to working with a black screen and computerised voice, than I would have expected, and the story outline is starting to take shape. They already have a fairly sound plot structure and almost every session, I'm tempted to ask them why they don't write the story themselves. They clearly have a great understanding of the English language and a solid knowledge of narrative structure. But I don't ask. It's none of my business. My business is writing the best damn book I can.

'It's important to me that there's no indication of which

person is doing the murders,' they tell me as we work together the following Monday evening. 'I want that to be the big reveal at the end.'

I get it. It's not a thriller if you can guess from page one who's doing the killing, but it does make it harder to write.

'I guess we'll need to use they/them pronouns throughout the murder scenes so we don't know who we are looking at,' I suggest. 'In terms of clothes, we could make them both monochrome in their dress choices too. Dark trainers, jogging bottoms, that kind of thing. Maybe just leave a couple of breadcrumbs for the readers. Not all will pick up on them, but those who do will love it.'

'If you think that will work, I will trust you.'

As well as not knowing who the murderer is, Dr B is insistent that each death will look innocuous and pass as either a suicide or an accident to the police, allowing the perpetrator to get away with it. Their plot currently includes an influencer's death by carbon monoxide poisoning, a nemesis being strangled in their home only for the perpetrator to set the scene so it looks like death by hanging, along with an electrocution, a house fire and a poisoning to cause a heart attack, although they have not yet decided who those deaths happen to. But while Dr B helps come up with the list, I'm the one who has to research how to write them to make them sound entirely believable. Which is what I spend most of the weekend doing.

'The band's got a gig in a beer garden this evening,' Duncan says as he brings me a cup of tea and places it on the corner of my desk on Sunday morning. 'I thought you might like to come.'

'Maybe,' I say, not even looking up from the screen as I reach out and take the mug. 'I guess I'll have to see how far through this I get. I really want to make this murder sound as believable as possible.' I take a sip of my drink, at which point, I finally look up at him. It's the strangulation that needs to look like a hanging and I've got to get down the nitty gritty with all the dirty details. 'If the police ever decide to go through our computer's search history, we're screwed. Just so you know.' I flash Duncan a quick smile, but he's slow to reciprocate.

'Are you sure you're not doing too much?' he says. 'You've barely been doing this a week, and I feel like it's taken over your life. You were still up when I came home last night and you're already up doing it again now. You'll burn yourself out if you're not careful.'

'I'll be fine. It'll slow down when I've got the research part done. This part is always the most intensive.'

'As long as you're sure?'

'I am.'

I say the words with such confidence, though I don't have a clue. This is my only experience of doing this type of thing, and while I know Professor Jarvis is there if I need any advice, I'd rather just get it all done with minimal fuss.

'Okay, well, maybe you can take a break for a bit and we could go for a walk or something?' Duncan says.

My instinct is to say no, but at the same moment, I feel a slight crick in my neck, probably from sitting in the same position for too long. If I don't move soon, I might seize up even more and then that'll make working a nightmare.

'A walk sounds like a great idea,' I tell him. 'Just as a quick one, though.'

40

It's around four in the afternoon when Dr B emails to say they want to put another session in.

'I might still be able to catch the end of your set,' I say to Duncan as he pouts. 'Remember, we used the money. I have to earn it now.'

'I know,' he sighs. 'Only the guys were talking about going for a couple of drinks afterwards. I was hoping we'd both be able to go, but are you still all right if I do? Even if you don't make it?'

'Of course I am.'

I reach up onto my tiptoes and kiss him lightly on the lips.

'Love you,' I say.

'Love you too. And I really don't mind coming back early if you want me to?'

'Honestly, the meetings are fine now. There's nothing to worry about.'

I'm not lying. Murders disguised as suicide are far from my ideal writing topic, but Dr B has kept everything focused on the story now, which is how it should have been from the beginning.

I think they understand that. I feel certain that we've turned a corner and everything from now on will be completely professional.

I open my computer and look at the latest task Dr B wanted – the first draft of the strangulation scene. To be honest, I didn't think I had it in me to write something like that, something so visceral, and perhaps I should be freaked out by how easily it came to me, but then again, there are thousands of thriller and crime authors out there; I guess it just takes a certain kind of person.

Confident that they're going to like my work so far, I log into the meeting and, for the first time since my interview, I actually feel a sense of optimism. Sure, Dr B is odd, but there are a lot of odd people out there. This one just happens to be paying me a lot of money.

They are normally so punctual, I have to have everything ready to start the moment I open the call, but at ten past eight, there's still no sign of them.

I send a quick email, checking I've got the time right, but there's no reply. I've just made the decision to give them two more minutes before I hang up when they finally click into the chat room. The voice is immediate.

'Sorry, I was just sorting something out.'

'No problem,' I reply, amazed at how accustomed I've become to the electronic voice. My ears seem to add inflections regardless of whether they are intended.

I know this is as much preamble as I'll get before they start, and just as predicted, they are straight in with the work.

'That first chapter you sent through was excellent,' they say. 'Perhaps a little lighter than I had envisioned it, but I assume that is because you plan on darkening the tone as the story progresses?'

'Yes, yes, absolutely,' I say. It's not exactly true. I already thought it was plenty dark enough; a man was murdered by being strangled after spending hours begging for his life. Then it was made to look like he had hung himself with a cord from a bathrobe. Worse still, the body was placed right by the kitchen window with the curtains wide open so that when morning came, passers-by would see it. Getting darker than that is something I'm going to have to work on, but Dr B is the one who has the ideas.

'Perhaps with the next murder, we hear a little more of their inner workings. Their indifference to what they're doing,' they suggest. 'Would that be possible? Maybe the true fear comes from how normal they are during the process. How steady their pulse is. How easily they justify their actions. How little they care?'

'Okay, yes. Of course.' I scribble the words *Make Darker?????* on my notepad beside me.

'And before I forget, I saw a young man who I thought was a perfect younger version of our male protagonist. I took a quick photograph. Is it okay if I send it across to you? I thought that might help to create a profile.'

Given how Dr B has not said anything about it since our first proper session, I assumed my suggestion about creating character profiles had been completely dismissed, so I'm pleased to see they're taking a little of my direction. Despite the initial massive bumps in the road, it's starting to feel like a genuinely collaborative process.

I wait for a moment, and then a message comes through. A second later, I open the attachment. It's a portrait photo, and even though there are several people within the frame, I know exactly which one I should be looking at. Bile stings the back of my throat as my stomach drops.

'Is this some kind of fucking joke?' I say. 'Why the fuck do you have a photo of my boyfriend?'

41

My whole body trembles so much, I can barely take a steady breath in. The entire scene makes me dizzy. It's a photo of Duncan. My Duncan, and he's with a girl who's holding her arm around his waist, gazing up at him adoringly.

'What the hell is this? Is this some kind of joke?' I repeat.

'Sorry, is something wrong?' The electronic voice causes every muscle in my body to tense. Blood pounds through my ears, rushing to my face with a burning heat.

'No, no, you don't get to do that. You don't get to use that fake voice. This is my boyfriend. This is a photograph of my boyfriend. You use your real voice right now or this is over. This project is done.'

'If you wish to dissolve the agreement of our—'

'Screw the contract. Screw the money. I don't care about any of it. If you do not speak to me in the next thirty seconds, then we are done. No, scrap that – five seconds. I don't have to deal with any of this. Shit. You're a fucking creep. I bet it was you following me, wasn't it? It wasn't Gloria at all. It was you. Fuck.' I go to hit my mouse when it happens.

'Francesca, wait.' For the first time, it's a real voice speaking to me. Not some electronic computation of human tones. It's a real voice. A male voice, and now he's started speaking, he's got more to say. 'What do you mean by you're being followed? I've never followed you,' he says. 'But if you think someone is, you should go to the police. I don't mind if you want to end the session tonight to do that. Your safety is most important.'

Wow, well, that was a perfect diversion technique, and it's not going to work on me. Not a chance.

'We're not ending this session until you tell me why you have a photograph of my boyfriend.'

His throat crackles.

'I'm sorry, I don't understand. You're telling me this photo I took is of your boyfriend?'

The voice is peculiarly quiet. As if it isn't sure how to speak. Or he doesn't want me to fully hear his voice.

My heart continues to drum against my chest as I struggle to look at the screen. Duncan is not the only person I recognise in the photograph. There are a couple of members of the band, like Tommy and Rafferty. The guys who sorted out this apartment for me. Who got all the furniture and tried to turn it into a home. Yet they're all laughing and joking, as if Duncan being with this woman is the most natural thing in the world.

'Why did you take this photo?' I say, hearing the cracks in my voice.

'I saw the guy playing in a band. I thought he was a perfect profile for Peter. I took his photo when he left the club. That's all there is to it.'

'I don't believe you.'

'I don't know what else to say. It's the truth.' He speaks in short sentences, which makes it hard to get a reading on his accent. Northern, perhaps.

'When did you take this?' I say. 'And where?'

'Saturday night, at a bar.' When he speaks now, it's almost like a West Country twang. He's changing his accent, or at least trying to, to make it so I can't work out where he's from. But why does that matter if I don't know him?

'Where was this music bar?'

'Liverpool.'

'Liverpool? No, that's not true. Duncan hasn't gone to Liverpool for years. He was gigging in London.'

'I don't know what to tell you. Maybe it's not your boyfriend. Maybe it's somebody different. This guy was definitely in Liverpool on Saturday when I took this photograph.'

'I don't believe you.'

Silence follows us. There's nothing more to be said.

'I'm sorry, Francesca, really, I am. I wouldn't have sent this photo if I didn't think it would be helpful to you. I swear. I would never do anything to jeopardise doing this project with you. It's going so well.'

He sounds earnest, but the accent is switching again.

'I need you to tell me everything. Right now.'

He coughs, a slight throat clearance, and I want to see his face more than ever before. I want to tell him to remove that screen he has placed between himself and the camera, but I know that if I do that, this will be over. He'll hang up and I'll never hear from him again, and I can't do that, because I need to learn the truth about whatever is going on with Duncan.

'There's really not that much to tell,' he says. 'I went to a music club in Liverpool with some friends. We go there often, but this band hadn't played there before. I saw the guy playing.' The way he speaks is so void of emotion I could still be talking to the computer. Is it because he's telling the truth, or because he's an expert liar? Either way, he seems to have settled on a West

Country accent, though from some of the inflections, I don't think it's genuine. 'He was the perfect vision of what I had for Peter, but I couldn't get a decent photograph of him with all the lights and stuff, so I waited until he came out of the club later. When I saw him there, I took this shot. That's it. That's all I've got.'

'Duncan was in Liverpool?' I say.

'Assuming this guy is your boyfriend. I mean, the light's not great. Maybe he just looks similar, right? I'm sure if he was in Liverpool, it'll be easy enough to find out.'

The way he's speaking, it's like he's trying to cover for Duncan. Like he feels sorry for my boyfriend, who's clearly lying to me, rather than feeling sorry for me.

'I think we need to stop this evening,' I say.

'Oh, but we still have a lot to get on with. I'll see you on Tuesday, same time?'

'We'll see,' I say.

A second later, I hang up.

42

I don't know how long I sit there, staring at the photo. There is no mistaking it. Sure, it's from a distance and the evening light adds a certain haze to the image, but it's the way his smile glances up at one side, ever so slightly, and the manner in which his hand is tucked into his jean pocket so his thumb slips into the belt loops. There is no mistaking that this is Duncan. My Duncan. With another girl's arm wrapped around his waist.

The realisation is dizzying. Nauseating.

I pick up my phone and check the time. Nine-thirty. They were finishing early tonight, weren't they? That was why he was planning on heading out for drinks with everyone afterwards. Unless, of course, that was just something to say: a ploy to throw me off his scent. It would make sense that he'd assume I wouldn't want to come out. I rarely do. My head's spiralling. I can feel it. I can feel myself going through all the reasons he might have been in Liverpool, or have had a girl's arm around his waist, the same way I tried to go through all the reasons my dad would shoot my mum. And each time, I came up empty, just like I'm doing now.

But this is different. Very different. This time, I have a way to find answers.

I open my phone to the location app we use to check where one another is, only to change my mind. The app doesn't hold data so all it would tell me is where he is now, and that's not the issue. The issue is who he's with and where he's been. According to the band's Facebook page, all their gigs this month have been in London. Then again, there have been a fair few occasions when other bands have cancelled and they've stepped in last minute, with no opportunity to advertise the change. Although that's always been local before, they are getting better known, and they could well have a connection up north I don't know about. What it comes down to is that there's no way I'm going to get any of the answers I want without confronting him.

I switch the phone screen over to messages.

> Have you been to Liverpool recently?

That's the text I send. I hope it seems innocuous enough, and if he's innocent, his answer will show it, and if he's not, well then, he's been rumbled. Immediately, the three dots of an impending message appear on the screen, and a second later, the text follows.

> Liverpool? Didn't we go there about two years ago? Why? Do you want to visit? It's meant to be really nice.

It's certainly not the message I'd expect a lying cheat to send, but then isn't that the whole point – if they're good enough liars, you don't notice.

> No reason. I'll talk to you later.

As I drop the phone onto the arm of the chair, Dr B's words flicker into my mind.

If he went to Liverpool, it would be easy enough to find out. That was what Dr B said. What did he mean by that? How would I know if somebody had been to a certain city? There was nothing on the bands page and he wouldn't have any train tickets; he'd have driven there. But would that leave some trail of evidence? His car doesn't have satnav, so he would have used his phone to get there. Or someone else's. That's possible too. He could have driven up with that girl after all. Maybe it isn't as easy as Dr B said. It's not like Liverpool monitors who goes in and out of the city. Or does it? A flutter of excitement sparks within me as that single thought has a knock-on effect. They may not monitor the people, but they might charge them if there's a toll road.

I open up my phone and quickly start googling toll roads by Liverpool. One comes up straight away: the Mersey Tunnel. I'm assuming that if Duncan was to go to Liverpool and back, he would want to do it the quickest way possible, and that would mean taking this route.

I go to the website for the toll road. According to what I read, you can prepay or pay after the event online. Online payments mean an email receipt, don't they?

Duncan and I don't hide passwords from one another. We use each other's accounts for different things and I've never thought twice about logging onto his emails to check when a parcel's being delivered or a bill's due.

'You don't have to do this,' I say to myself as I click onto his profile. 'You could just ask him.'

I know I could, but then he could just lie.

The photo is only one bit of evidence, and it's not enough. I need something concrete. I need to know if he was actually in Liverpool.

I consider scrolling down his emails when I change my mind and hit the search bar at the top instead. *Mersey Tunnel*. Those two words are all I need to type. One way or another, I'll get my answer.

My breath catches as I click enter and wait for the answer to appear.

Mersey Tunnel toll. There are two results. And I hit the top one. Tears flood my eyes.

Duncan used the toll road on Saturday. Duncan is lying to me.

43

I don't bother going to bed. There's no point; I won't go to sleep. I know that. Right now, my body is buzzing and my head is swimming with questions that don't have any answers. There's no way it could be a coincidence that Dr B chose my boyfriend, Duncan, to photograph? And even if it is, it doesn't change the fact that Duncan has lied to me.

As I lie awake, I try to play devil's advocate. Could this just have been a way for Dr B to get under my skin? Like the way he asked me what I was most ashamed of in the interview? It's not beyond the realm of possibility, but he must have known who Duncan was. I just can't believe it's random. And he can't have faked Duncan being in Liverpool.

I wish there was drink in the house. Strong drink. I need something to calm me, although right now, I don't know what is causing me the most distress: Duncan or Dr B.

I know Dr B researches the people he works with. He said that to me from the very beginning. So, what if that research extended to Duncan? What if he's known since before we even began this project together that Duncan was cheating on me, and he's only now plucked up the courage to tell me the truth? It feels unnervingly possible. Particularly with the way he switched to his natural voice for the first time. He didn't want me to hang up. It was like he didn't expect me to be as upset as I was, but then that would mean he hadn't known who Duncan was. And even if he had, what would he gain from telling me this? It's not like I'd be able to spend more time on the project if we split up; Duncan and I barely have time to talk to one another as it is. So why would he do it unless his overall aim was to help me? It's a constant back and forth in my head, only there are no answers, just more questions, and each one is leaving me more confused.

I know if I called Duncan, he'd come home, but I'm not sure that's what I want. I want him to act on his own devices and see where we end up. Still, around 1 a.m., my mind starts racing even faster. Duncan's arrival time is imminent, assuming he comes home tonight. For all I know, he could be getting in at three or four each night. Staying out as late as possible to spend time with this other woman and slipping in while I'm fast asleep and none the wiser. Knowing this makes me feel sick.

As I sit there in the armchair, I hear footsteps padding up the stairs and know that any second now, our front door is going to go. When it finally opens, I don't waste any time.

'You're home later than I thought you'd be,' I say.

'Jeez, Frankie.' Duncan jumps visibly before he places his bass down by the door. 'What the hell are you doing hiding in the dark?'

'I wanted to wait up for you.'

He walks across to the chair and kisses me on the forehead. He smells of pubs – of beer and sweat – but I can't help wondering why he doesn't kiss me on the lips. Is it because he's worried I'll taste someone else?

There's a slight swagger to his step as he moves back. Duncan never gets drunk. After his brother was killed, for years, he stopped drinking altogether, but sometimes he has one or two beers when he's out now, if he knows there's zero chance of him driving. The limited intake means it always shows.

'Please don't tell me you've been working all this time,' he says. 'You're going to make yourself ill at this rate.'

'I just wanted to ask you again about Liverpool—'

'Wait a minute. Do you want to go to Liverpool? Is that what this is about? Only do we have to talk about it now? I'm knackered.'

'No, you misunderstand me. I should probably have said I know about Liverpool.'

A large crease appears between his brows as his confusion deepens. 'What do you mean, you know about Liverpool? Sorry, babe, I'm knackered. You're going to have to be a little clearer than that. Do you want to go, or not?'

'I know that you went, Duncan. I know that you've been lying to me. I know about her.'

'Her?' He shakes his head. I have to admit, he's doing a damn good job of lying. It makes me wonder how long he's been doing it for. 'Who are you on about?'

I'm ready for this moment. In two strides, I'm across the room and beside my desk, where I flick up my laptop screen. The image is there in full size: Duncan's arms wrapped around a stunning, leggy blonde. 'I know about her.'

Duncan picks up the laptop, stares at the photo. 'Who sent this to you?'

'It doesn't matter who sent it to me.'

'No, it matters who sent it to you because whatever you think's going on in this photograph, you're mistaken.'

'So this isn't the girl that you've been seeing behind my back?'

'What? No! This is just some weird woman who ran out and

wrapped her arms around me after a gig last week. I just assumed she was completely drunk. Most of them are.'

I shake my head, unable to stop the bitter laugh from escaping between my lips. It scares me to think how I would have believed him. I'm sure of it. Only I take the computer from him and flick to another screen. 'Okay, so say you're telling the truth about that, then explain this. Explain what you were doing in Liverpool three days ago, when you told me you haven't been there for years.'

This time, Duncan takes the laptop from me and moves over to the armchair, where he takes a seat, still staring at the screen. 'I have no idea what you're saying here. What is this?'

'This is your email account, Duncan. These are your emails and that is a receipt with your car registration on saying that you paid for the toll to go to Liverpool on Saturday. There is one there, and another, six hours apart. Why would that happen if you hadn't been to Liverpool?'

'I don't know. Perhaps it's just a mistake. Maybe someone put in the wrong email address. I'm sure it happens.'

'What, they put in the wrong email address that happens to coincide with your exact car registration? And on the same day I was told that you were up in Liverpool?'

If he'd just said he was doing a last-minute gig with the guys, and he hadn't wanted to worry me because he was going to be so far away, I would have at least wanted to believe him. But the way he's denying even going there when I have the evidence in front of me is infuriating.

He slams the laptop closed as he glowers at me. 'Can you at least tell me who is telling you these lies? Because it's not true.'

'Well, the evidence is pretty damning.'

'Your evidence is fake, sorry, Frankie. Look, I don't know what's going on, but I promise you, I haven't been to Liverpool and I'm not cheating on you. I wouldn't do that, you know that. Will you please just tell me who's saying this stuff to you?'

My back teeth grind together with so much force, I can feel the vibrations through my skull.

'So that's it. You're telling me none of this is true?'

'That's what I'm telling you.'

I shake my head. Surely he should try to come up with some explanation. But the way he's acting, it's like he doesn't even care. That he thinks he can lie straight to my face and get away with it.

'You know what? You should sleep out here,' I say. 'Or give that girl a call. I'm sure she's got room in her bed for you. You probably know where it is.'

With that, I walk into the bedroom and slam the door shut.

44

I don't fall asleep straight away; I can't, mainly because I can hear Duncan pacing around. He puts some food in the microwave, then moves back to the living room. The chairs we have are less than ideal for sleeping in, but he's lucky I didn't kick him out of the apartment. Then again, part of me thought he would go anyway. I think I want him to. I wanted him to leave when he thought I was asleep so I could follow his location on the phone and catch him in the act, but I guess he's too smart to fall for that.

At some point, all the sounds stop, and I guess he must have fallen asleep. My body is so tired. My muscles feel double their normal weight, but every time I close my eyes, my brain starts buzzing away again. Has he really been that good a liar our entire relationship? Because I would've bet my life he was telling the truth. But that's the whole thing with great liars, isn't it? You do believe them. That's why they get away with it.

At some point, I fall asleep, because I wake up when I feel a shift in the mattress. A weight on the side causes it to sink down and me to slip to the side. When I open my eyes, Duncan is sitting there with a cup of tea in his hands, which he holds out to me. On the bedside table is my phone. I don't remember it being there before I went to bed, so I guess I left it in the living room and Duncan brought it in.

'I was worried you were going to oversleep and miss your morning lectures.'

I don't know why I thought he'd be gone. Perhaps that was just wishful thinking. I was hoping he wouldn't draw this out longer than we need to, but a quick glance at my phone tells me he's right. It's already twenty to nine. Without a word, I shift my legs around him so that I can stand. As I make my way to my pile of clothes, he speaks again.

'Frankie, we need to talk about last night.'

'No, we don't,' I say as I slip on a top. 'I don't have time. I've got a lecture.'

He puts the tea down and walks towards me.

'We need to sort out what's going on first. Lectures can wait.'

With a rush of anger, I spin around and lock my eyes onto his. 'That's where you're wrong. There's nothing to sort out between us. I no longer trust you. That's what it comes down to. And that's not something you can sort out over a cup of tea, Duncan.'

He takes an audible breath in, which he lets out in a long blow.

'Frankie, I don't know what's going on with you, but you're worrying me.'

'Really?' I arch an eyebrow. He's the one who gets caught cheating, and he's worried about me? Funny that.

'Yes. Since you spoke to Gloria, you've been slipping. Surely you can see that.'

'Slipping?' The second eyebrow joins the first.

He shakes his head. 'I don't know what to call it, but you

haven't been yourself. You've been nervous and withdrawn. And you've been lying to me. I know you're still ringing hospitals. Still trying to find her.'

I scoff. A bitter laugh catches in my throat.

'Trying to work out what happened to my friend is hardly lying.'

'It's lying by omission. Or near enough. Same as the way you didn't tell me that some famous writer came onto campus and started yelling at you. You weren't keeping that from me?'

I feel the colour drain from my cheeks.

'How do you know that?'

'Heidi messaged me. She's worried about you. She says she's hardly seen anything of you recently. And that when she has, you haven't seemed yourself.'

I am utterly gobsmacked, though why, I'm not sure. Heidi was probably just trying to get some extra info on the apartment move and knew she wouldn't get a house-warming invitation through me. No doubt that's why she rang Duncan. That, and she thought she could stir a bit of shit into the pot too.

'What the hell would Heidi know? She's too busy fucking our bloody professor.'

He steps back, his eyes narrowing slightly. 'Surely you can hear what you sound like, Frankie? This isn't you. I don't know what's going on, but this isn't like you.'

'I'm doing what *you* asked me to do!' I lift my hands in the air with exasperation. 'You were the one who wanted me to take this job so we had money to move out. Who wanted me to work for—'

'So that's where the photo came from? That's who's told you I'm cheating on you. That fucking Dr B freak?'

'Why's he a freak? Because he wants me to know the truth? Because he's trying to make me see what a liar you are?'

'Frankie, I'm not. I swear. Ask any of the band. Ask Tommy. Please, this isn't like you. You're scaring me.' He inches towards me, but I flick him away with my hand.

'No, no. I'm gonna get to the bottom of this. I am. Stay away from me. You hear me? Stay away.'

45

There have been a number of photos printed of me in which I am crying in public. Obviously, that was the image the press wanted to portray. Every time they posted a photo, it would have the same type of headline: *Broken Daughter Left, Tragic Second Victim of Murder-Suicide Lives On.*

But today, as I head onto campus, I don't even try to stop the tears from rolling down my cheeks. And the truth is, even with Duncan, I wasn't naïve enough to believe in the happily ever after that books and films want us to think exist. I didn't believe that we would get to the end of our relationship and grow old without the slightest issue. But I imagined we'd have at least five or ten years ahead of us. Maybe until he wanted someone with a bit more spark. Maybe until we came to that well-known crunch point of children and discovered we didn't want the same things after all. I suppose if I'm honest with myself, I'd imagined dozens of ways he might have ended things, but never like this. Never because of his lying. Of his manipulating me.

I'm so lost in my thoughts that I don't even notice when Heidi slips into the seat next to me, blocking the way out.

'Hey.' She speaks so casually. Clearly, she thinks I don't know about her talking to Duncan behind my back. 'I messaged you over the weekend. All that stuff with Rupert was horrid. I thought you and Duncan might have liked to come over for a drink. You know, as a distraction. I've got all these whiskies that some brand wants me to do a promotion for, and I thought you could help me try them. I really don't get the whisky thing, but thankfully Ivor was there. He's really knowledgeable about things like that. It's such a shame I can't use any of the photos I took of him on my page. He has a real gravitas, you know. Here, look at these.'

I don't have any desire to see selfies of Professor Jarvis drinking whisky while Heidi kisses his cheek, but I don't have a choice as she shoves the photos directly under my nose. She seems to have forgotten her previous comments about needing to be discreet. Then again, with the way he's smiling and his fashionable flat cap – that was undoubtedly Heidi's choice – I'm not even sure I'd recognise the man as Professor Jarvis if I didn't know.

'Gorgeous, aren't we? It would make such a perfect profile picture, right? But that's just the burden of being in a relationship like ours. You have no idea how difficult it is to finally find the man of your dreams and not be able to share it with the world.'

She lets out a sigh, oblivious to the look of contempt I know I'm displaying on my face. I swear the lady at the checkout in our local supermarket asks me more questions about myself than Heidi does. She continues to flick through the photos and despite my better judgement, I can't help looking. She's a damn good photographer, even if most of it is selfies. She knows how to use the light and structure the compositions so her images are consistently striking. Still, I'm about to force my eyes away and open up my laptop when she swipes to a photo of them at a park. My hand reaches out and grabs hers.

'That's Phil,' I say, looking at a man in the background of the image. He's a fair distance away from the camera, but he's staring straight at it and perfectly in focus.

'Phil? Your housemate? The pot-smoking one.'

'Yeah. I didn't think he knew what a park was.'

He's dressed all in black, which isn't unusual for Phil, but there's something unnerving about the way he's staring into the camera. It's as if he wants us to notice him there. That's what I think, anyway, although Heidi merely shrugs.

'I get so many photobombers. They want to get onto my page,' she sighs, before moving on to show me yet more photos of her and Ivor.

Thankfully, Dr Morley is heading to the front of the room, meaning the lecture's about to start and Heidi has to be quiet. Still, it doesn't stop her flicking through several more photos before she finally puts her phone away.

Heidi is annoyingly noisy in lectures. She doesn't speak or interrupt, but she makes constant umms and ahhing sounds and asks double the number of questions that anyone else does. I'm sure she thinks it makes her look intelligent. Like she understands everything the lecturer is saying, but that's not the case. It just looks like she has an inability to sit in silence.

The lecture drags, and several times, I glance at the clock, only to be surprised by how slowly time is moving. I know I snapped at Duncan for letting me sleep, but I honestly feel like all those extra hours were detrimental. I feel even more tired than before I went to bed, and that's saying something.

While I'm busy trying to stifle a yawn, the back door to the lecture hall creaks open. I use the distraction to stretch my jaw fully and pull in a large lungful of air, though before I'm done, the voice speaks.

'Sorry to interrupt your lecture, Dr Morley.'

I don't need to look around to know Professor Jarvis's voice, and neither does Heidi. Her face beams as she turns towards him. Her fingers twitch in a small wave she wrongly assumes is subtle. And I don't doubt the professor can see, as he's looking straight at her.

'Professor Jarvis, this is a surprise,' Dr Morley says.

'Yes, sincere apologies. But I need to have a word with Francesca Crawford. Now, please.'

46

I hate that I am right at the front of the lecture hall. I can feel every pair of eyes looking at me. See all the inquisitive glances and feel the question of what I've done whirring through their minds.

As I stand up and gather my things, I glance to my side and see Heidi doing exactly the same. Is it an act of solidarity? Quite possibly. Or maybe she already knows why he wants to speak to me. Either way, as I walk out of the lecture theatre, she is there right by my side.

My stomach is churning as we step into the hallway, though it's not until he's pushed the lecture hall door closed that Professor Jarvis speaks.

'I'm sorry about the interruption,' he says, looking at me, but Heidi cuts in before I can speak.

'Ivor, are you okay? You don't look right. Has something happened?' Her sycophantic tone makes my skin crawl, but I have to admit she's right. He looks unnaturally sallow. Especially compared to those photos where he was drinking whiskey.

Rather than replying immediately, Professor Jarvis presses his lips together.

'I'm sorry, Heidi, but I need to speak to Francesca alone right now. It's a private matter.'

'A private matter?' She lets out a slight titter of disbelief. 'Don't be silly. Frankie doesn't mind me being here. Do you, Frankie?'

I don't know how I'm meant to reply to the question, given that I don't know why I'm there. But thankfully, before I'm forced to think of an answer, Professor Jarvis responds.

'You should probably get back to your lecture,' he says to her. 'You don't want to miss any more.'

Her lips purse, and she looks as if she's going to object again, but then her eyes narrow as her gaze shifts between me and Professor Jarvis.

'I guess I should leave you two to whatever this private matter of yours is,' she says, before turning on her heel and swinging the door to the lecture hall back open. As I watch her go, her intonation of the word 'private' rings in my ear. She couldn't possibly have been implying that she thought there was something going on between us, could she? That's ludicrous. But maybe not to her. I wonder if there's something I should do, but I don't know what, and before I can say anything, Professor Jarvis speaks again.

'Perhaps you should take a seat,' he says, gesturing to a row of chairs next to the wall. Between lectures, they're always full, but now everybody is in class, they're entirely empty. For a second, I just stare at them. I'm not sure I want to sit down, but I don't want to refuse either, so I do as requested and a moment later, Professor Jarvis takes a place in the chair directly next to me. It's unnervingly close, but it's not like I can move away now. Whatever this is, I need to get it over and done with as soon as possible. I didn't notice until now, but he's been holding a newspaper beneath his arm the entire time, which he pulls out and places on his lap. I'm sure he isn't about to open it up and start casually reading next to me, but it feels like he might.

'Francesca. Frankie,' he says, almost unable to meet my eye. 'I didn't want you to hear about this through any other route, and I know after the incident last week, there'll probably be some thoughts running through your head, but I want you to know, I want to promise you, this incident has absolutely nothing to do with you whatsoever.'

'Incident?' I'm confused. I have no idea what he's going on about. 'What incident? What happened?'

He draws in a deep breath before he gives me the answer.

'It's Rupert,' he says finally. 'Rupert Fitzherbert. He was found dead this morning. He killed himself.'

47

Silence fills the hallway. The words are taking too long to comprehend. It's not just that Rupert's dead, is it? That's not why Professor Jarvis wanted to speak to me alone like this.

He was found this morning. That was how he said it. *Found*. So he didn't die this morning. He died…

'After he came here, after he found out I got the job, is that why he did it? Because he didn't get the money and he needed it. He needed that job.'

'No, absolutely not,' Professor Jarvis assures me, reaching out and pressing his hand on my arm. 'That's what I wanted to say to you. I think his coming here to the university was a last cry for help. He needed someone to notice how bad things had got for him. And I should have seen it. It's on me. I don't want you to bear any of the weight of this, you understand? It is not on you. None of it. Rupert was a troubled man for many years.'

I nod, but everything feels numb. Whether it was a last cry for help or not, he still came to me with it. There's a good chance that Professor Jarvis and I were the last people who spoke to him, and the words we used weren't exactly pleasant.

'The writing community are holding drinks tonight,' the professor continues. 'You will receive an invitation from the ghost-writing company. I understand if you don't want to attend. If you would rather avoid the situation. It's entirely up to you. There will be no judgement from anyone.'

Again, I feel my chin nodding, but I'm not sure why.

'I've got a meeting with Dr B tonight,' I say. 'We have some things to work through. Is that okay?'

'Of course.' He draws in another breath. 'Well, I'm glad I got the opportunity to tell you. I didn't want you to find out some other way. Are you sure you're okay? I've got a secret stash of whiskey in my office if you think a dram might help. Quite a lot, actually.'

I can't help but let out a laugh, though it doesn't stop a tear trickling down my cheek.

'Is it in there?' I gesture to the paper on his lap. 'Is it already in the news?'

He nods. 'It's not a pretty read, I'm afraid.' His lips press tightly together before he speaks again. 'Why don't you go home?' he suggests. 'Take the rest of the morning off. I'm sure someone can send the lecture notes through to you.'

I go to smile, then shake my head. 'Honestly, I think being here is the best thing,' I say. 'Going home sounds like a nice idea, but it would mean catching up on lecture notes, and I don't have the time to do that.'

'Okay, well maybe just sit here for a while then. Let's be honest, you're not missing anything in Professor Morley's lecture. They've not updated their script for the best part of a decade.'

I allow myself another light chuckle, which fades into the silence as I sit here. Is this what other people's lives are like? Constantly interrupted by tragedy? I don't know. It's not as if I even knew Rupert. I don't know why I'm feeling this heavy weight of guilt festering inside me.

I can't be held responsible for not foreseeing his actions. Just like I can't be held responsible for my father's actions. Maybe that's why it hurts so badly.

It's only when the door to the lecture hall opens and Heidi steps outside that I realise how long we've been sitting there together.

'Everything sorted?' she asks. 'Oh, it looks like I'm interrupting.' There's an unusual iciness to her voice. That's when I notice Professor Jarvis's hand is still on my arm. I gently free myself.

'Not at all,' I say before standing up and looking back at the professor. 'You understand that I won't come tonight?'

'Of course.'

'May I... could I please...?'

I glance down at the paper in his hands, and there's no need for me to say any more.

'You might find it upsetting, but I guess if I don't give you this copy, you'll just find another, won't you?'

'Most probably.'

His eyes lock onto mine, and their sadness is momentarily clouded by something else. Something darker. He looks almost scared. 'Frankie, be careful,' he says as he hands me the paper. His lips hover millimetres apart, as if they want to say more, and in that second, his fear is so raw. It's like it's burning him from within. But in a blink, that moment's gone. He's forcing a smile to his mouth, and the same sad glint has returned to his eyes. 'Take care of yourself, won't you?'

'I will,' I say, not sure why the hairs on the back of neck have all risen. As I walk away, I can feel Heidi's glare boring into me, but I don't have the energy to care.

I take the paper straight outside and find a quiet bench to sit down on. I don't know why I need to read it so badly. It's not like it will change anything that's happened, but I want to see the words in black and white. Understand how it happened. Maybe learn some more about this man who might still be alive if I hadn't got the job he needed to get his finances in order.

His money problems are mentioned in the first part of the article, along with his divorce, dismissal from the university and the dropping by his agent, but it's when I reach the part of his death that the goosebumps appear on my arms.

A neighbour saw his silhouette by the window in the early morning and thought nothing of it, but when she saw it again, in the same place later in the day, she rang the police thinking the behaviour was strange. When the police entered the house, they found him with a dressing-gown cord wrapped around his neck. Suicide – that's what they have said. The word is used at least three times in the article, but it's not that. It's murder. I know, because the description is so familiar, I could have written it myself. I pretty much did.

48

I scrunch the paper up under my arms as I race back into the English building. This is Dr B's doing. What happened to Rupert is what I wrote as the nemesis's death. It's the second murder in the book, and it happens after the influencer was murdered by carbon monoxide. There is no way this is a coincidence. Everything started falling apart when Dr B came into my life. Gloria, Duncan cheating and lying. Fuck. I need to stop him before he hurts anyone else. Before he hurts me.

I don't slow my pace as I take the steps two at a time, already knowing exactly which door I'm heading for.

As it comes into view, I don't even think about knocking – perhaps that's silly considering what I saw last time – but maybe I assume it can't get any worse than that.

I can hear voices coming from inside the room. As I swing open the door to Professor Jarvis's room, I see why. He's conducting a seminar with PhD students. Whatever he was saying, he cuts it off mid-sentence as he sees me there.

'Francesca,' he says, 'is everything okay?'

'No, no, it's not. I need to speak to you.'

He looks from me to the class and back again. 'Can it wait? This finishes in ten minutes.'

'No, no, it can't.'

I try to convey my urgency through my eyes. It's all I've got, short of begging.

He chews down on his bottom lip, and I assume he's going to tell me I have to wait, but he doesn't. Instead, he looks to his class.

'Well, we've pretty much come to the end, anyway. You know what you've got to work on. Please, read those texts. It will benefit you. Off you go. And make sure you're writing every day. It's a muscle, ladies and gentlemen. Train it.'

I see all the looks they exchange, the whispers they share as they walk past me, but I don't care. I hold my head up and focus on Dr Jarvis.

The room is finally empty. I step inside and slam the paper down on his desk.

'I wrote this.'

'Sorry?' he says, squinting slightly to read the print. 'Francesca, I told you, Rupert had—'

'Issues. Gambling problems. I know, Dr B told me that. But I wrote this. You don't understand. He made me write the scene. He made me write a scene where an entitled, middle-aged, white man was murdered by strangulation in his kitchen, then made to look like he'd hung himself with his bathrobe. That's what happened here.'

Dr Jarvis remains silent as he scans down the page.

'Francesca, I understand this must be upsetting—'

'You're not listening to me. Dr B is a murderer. I'm sure of it. Please, I need to know who he is. If I'm right, I'm in serious danger. I can't do this bullshit anonymous crap any more. I have to know.'

At this, Professor Jarvis closes the paper and looks at me.

'Francesca, I'm sorry that you're having such a difficult time with this. If you want me to talk to the company, then—'

'I want you to listen to me!' I shout.

A second later, I close my eyes and draw a long inhale through my nose, though it does little to calm me. My hands are still clenched at my sides. 'Please, please listen to me. I already told you that he knew things about me, didn't I? Well, I think he heard about what Rupert did, coming in and yelling at me, and he killed him because of it.'

'Francesca, is everything all right?' I turn around to see Heidi staring at us, her face uncharacteristically wrinkled with concern. 'What are you doing here? You look upset. Ivor, is everything okay?'

That's when I realise she's not looking at me with concern at all. It's jealousy. Paranoia. And I don't have time for it.

'This doesn't concern you, Heidi,' I say. 'Please, could you just get out?'

'Has something—'

'Will you just fuck off?' I hear my words resonate around the office. A look of shock shines on Heidi's face, but I don't pay it any attention. Instead, I clench my fists at my side as I draw a long breath in. 'Look, I've got enough to deal with right now. I need to talk to Professor Jarvis. Alone.'

As I finish speaking, Professor Jarvis clears his throat. 'Francesca, I understand that this is very upsetting. Go home. Take a couple of days if you need it. Rest.'

'I can't take a couple of days; my scholarship depends on my attendance!'

'I can see you need to get yourself well. You're clearly struggling.'

'Of course I'm struggling. I'm working for a bloody murderer.'

Why won't they listen to me? Why won't they believe me?

This is just like before. When everybody refused to accept that my father hadn't killed my mother. He didn't do it, just like Rupert didn't hang himself. But how the hell am I going to make them see that?

'Fine, screw you,' I say, picking up the paper and snatching it out from under Professor Jarvis's nose. 'I'm right; you'll see I'm right. You just better hope you're not the next person on his list.'

'I'm sure whatever it is, you're just over reacting,' Heidi comments as I pass her. 'It won't be anywhere near as bad as you think. These things rarely are.'

Given what she knows about me and my past, I can't believe she'd make such a flippant remark. Using every bit of self-control I have, I turn to look her straight in the eye.

'Well if anyone else ends up dead, I'll tell than you thought I was over-reacting. Remember that.'

49

As I storm out of Professor Jarvis's office, I hear the door close behind me. No doubt Heidi is whispering in his ear, telling him about my past and how there's a reason for my instability – if she hasn't told him that already. But when I look back at those times, even the darkest months, I never considered myself unstable. Lonely, yes; convinced my father wasn't guilty, yes. But not unstable. Just like I'm not unstable now. But I'm the only person who's actually able to see what's going on.

My feet are moving, but it's only when I'm on the downstairs corridor that I realise I'm heading to the library. I don't know why. I don't want quiet. I want to scream. I can feel in my bones that I'm right about this and Dr B is behind Rupert's death. But how the hell do I prove that to anyone? It's not like Dr B is going to confess to the murder. Unless...

I stop where I am, only a few feet away from a table and chair, but I can't sit down. My mind is too busy to think about walking any further. There's no denying Dr B is insane. Employing me when I'm completely unqualified to do the job, telling me about Duncan cheating and then Rupert's death so soon after he came onto campus to abuse me, but none of these things have put me in danger. If anything, it feels like Dr B is trying to protect me, rather than hurt me.

So maybe there is a way I can get what I want after all.

I pull out my phone and write the quickest message I can, not even reading it through before I hit send.

> I want to speak to you. Now.

I don't know what Dr B does or who he is, but I get the feeling that I'm right about this. His employment of me wasn't random and if people want evidence that he's behind Rupert's death, then maybe I can get it for them. Maybe I can get a confession.

My hands are trembling as I stare at my phone. There's no reason he'll see the message straight away. He probably has a job. He must do to earn the type of money he's paying me. And yet as I walk to take a seat, my phone buzzes.

With my throat growing drier by the second, I open a message that's even briefer than mine.

> I have five minutes.

50

'I need this room; it's an emergency!' I don't know who the girl working away alone in the study room is and I don't care. I need somewhere private to speak to Dr B and hers is the only room with one person in. She looks at me with wide eyes and annoyance, and when she opens her mouth, I'm almost sure she's going to refuse to move. So I don't give her the chance.

'Don't cross me today,' I growl.

I've never thought of myself as intimidating. Not in the slightest, but from the way she grabs her things and scuttles out of the room, I must have some hint of scariness about me. Either that or maybe I come across as insane.

As soon as she's gone, I close the door, draw the blind and get my laptop out.

It's already been two minutes since I got the message from Dr B, so I have to hope he wasn't being literal, but I can't open the meeting link until I've got my phone set up.

I open the voice-memo app, hit record then open the link.

Dr B is already there waiting for me.

'Francesca, is everything all right?'

He's using the computerised voice again, and it's annoying. I was hoping that now I'd heard his actual voice, we'd be past that. Apparently not.

'Rupert Fitzherbert,' I say. 'The writer that you interviewed for my job. They found his body this morning. He died by suicide.'

'Really? Well, some people don't realise how precious life is,' he says. It's not the type of response I expected, but given how he spoke about Rupert previously, I'm not sure I should be surprised. Still, there is only a slight pause before the next response comes through. 'Is that why you wanted to speak? Did you want to cancel this evening's session?'

I clear my throat with a cough.

'Not exactly. His death. He hung himself with the cord from his bathrobe, although the police found his body in the kitchen. By the window.'

It might not be a straight accusation, but he knows what I'm saying. My pulse quickens as I wait for him to respond.

'Is that right?' he says after a slight pause.

'It is. It sounds familiar, doesn't it?'

This time, the pause stretches out, and in the silence, I hear the hammering of my pulse. I don't want to ask him outright. I want him to just tell me, but it's not going to happen. He's waiting for me to say the words. Waiting for me to ask the question. I can feel it. Tension spreads through my muscles, tightening and tightening until I can bear it no more.

'Did you do it?' I say, when I can hold it in no longer. 'Did you kill him? Did you murder Rupert and make it look like suicide?'

There's nothing. No breathing. No smacking of lips. Then finally, his voice comes through.

'You do what it takes to protect the people you love.'

The shock of hearing the confession causes a gasp to flee from my lungs, but before I can even cover my mouth, the line goes dead.

51

I'm in no doubt now. Dr B is a murderer, but that line, about protecting the people he loves, does that mean me? That was how it felt, but then, how could I have felt anything when the voice was spoken through a computer? There was no emotion. No intonation, so is that just what I want to think? Why would anyone want to think someone murdered for them? No one in their right mind would want that, surely?

As I go to leave, I remember the recording on the computer. I play back the few seconds only for the disappointment to strike me like a bullet. It's a recording on a phone of a computer voice. There's nothing identifiable. If I'd taken a video of the conversation coming from the computer, maybe that would be something, but this... I could have been having a conversation with myself while I got the computer to replay the answers. That's what the police will say. It's not proper evidence.

'Fuck!' I scream as I slam my fist down on the table so hard, the blinds shake. 'Fuck!'

I drop my hands onto my head. That can't have been for nothing. There has to be more to it. I have to have learned something I didn't know before, so what is it? He loves me? He killed Rupert because he wants to protect me? That can't be a serious clue, can it? Not when the only person who ever says they love or want to protect me is Duncan. And it couldn't be him, could it?

The thought makes the hairs rise on the back of my neck. Twenty-four hours ago and I wouldn't have thought he would ever cheat on me or lie about going somewhere like Liverpool, but all the evidence shows me he has. So what else has he lied about?

As I ask myself the question, another realisation draws all the heat away from my body.

Duncan's never been there when I've spoken to Dr B. He's offered to stay with me, but I've always said no, just like he would have assumed I'd do. Not once, out of every one of the meetings we've had, has Duncan been in the same building as me, for even a single minute.

My breaths are growing shallower as I struggle to accept what I'm telling myself, but the truth is, there's only one person who would kill to protect me, and all the evidence right now is pointing to him.

Duncan is Dr B. Duncan is a murderer.

52

The more I think about it, the more things make sense. Duncan's always said that his parents refused to talk about his brother because of the upset, but what if that's not it? What if he never lost his brother at all? What if the manipulation began right at the very beginning of our relationship? He has some photos of his brother, sure, but they could be of anyone. Why did I not consider that before? They could be photos of friends, cousins. Anyone. Fuck, who the hell am I living with?

Rather than deepening my panic, this new piece of knowledge gives me a strange sense of calm. I just need to prove something. Something that shows Duncan isn't who he says he is. Once I've got that, it should be a whole lot easier to convince people that Duncan is responsible for Rupert's murder. I just need evidence.

The word is like a light switch in my head: *evidence*. That's what I couldn't find when it came to my parents' deaths. No forced entries, a gun in my father's name even though he was against guns. Nothing the police would look straight at. I've got the photo and the toll receipt, of course, but they're not enough.

Nowhere near. Other than proving Duncan's a lying boyfriend. I need something that shows he's really behind this. Or at least that he's been manipulating me for far longer than I've been calling him Mr B. Something that links him to the ghost-writing company or Rupert would be a silver bullet, but if I can just find evidence that his brother never existed, that would be something. Finally, for the first time in days, I have a focus.

I don't even bother going as far as the library. Instead, I sit down in the corridor and open up my phone. A quick Google search should tell me everything I need to know. As I type in the name Duncan gave me for his brother and the words *killed by drunk driver*, it strikes me as strange that I've never done it before. That I've just taken him entirely at face value, believing every word he said. No wonder I was such an easy target.

I hit send and find several newspaper articles on the first page, along with a series of photos, some of which I've already seen from Duncan. The moment I open up a site, I can see this route was a bust.

> Sixteen-year-old local lad killed by drunk driver. Leaves behind brother and grieving parents.

It's all there. The pang of disappointment is palpable. Duncan was telling the truth. A slight bitter laugh escapes my mouth. How much must a person have messed with your head that you're hoping they lied about their dead brother? I guess as much as Duncan has messed with mine.

As I slip my phone into my pocket, I refuse to let the disappointment settle. This was just one route of evidence. There have to be others. Something that links him to the ghost-writing or Rupert. Those would be silver bullets. If I can find something there, people will have to listen to me. Not just people – the police. But there's no way I'm going to find any of that out on a basic internet search, which means only one thing: I need to head back to the apartment.

I glance my phone, which tells me it's ten-thirty. Duncan's routine is erratic. Sometimes, he leaves early, either for band practice or a music lesson, but sometimes, he's home until mid-afternoon. The last thing I want is to give him more time to get rid of evidence – after all, he already made one slip-up by not deleting those receipts – but he mustn't think I'm onto him either and that might happen if I come back to the house unexpectedly. The best thing I can do is wait until the end of my lectures, then I'll leave here, head back to the apartment, and go through everything – his computer, the boxes of his stuff. Fingers crossed he'll be out well into the evening, and even if he's not, I can just say I'm unpacking. It's not a great plan, but it's a start, and that will have to do.

53

By the time I leave, my skin is itching with nerves. All afternoon, there's been one issue that's been pestering me: the photo. Duncan sending me the photo of him with that girl – while pretending to be Dr B – would make sense if he'd wanted to end things. Maybe he's been wanting to end things for a while but wasn't sure how to do it. By sending the evidence of him cheating, he'd be almost certain that I would break up with him and he wouldn't have to do the deed himself. Cowardly, yes, but I can see it making sense. Only he didn't seem to want to break up. He was insistent that it wasn't true, so if that's the case, then is his only aim to make me think I'm going mad? Maybe. Maybe I can use that.

I also can't overlook the fact that he killed Rupert directly after he found out he'd come onto campus and hurled abuse at me. The fact that Duncan would do that shows me that however twisted a man he is, he cares about me. That's good to know. Important. Hopefully, using that with the knowledge that I'm not actually losing my mind might be how I'll trap him.

My heart is pounding against my ribs as I slip the key into the lock. I haven't checked his location to see if Duncan is in now or not, but I get my answer straight away as I open the door and he stands up from the armchair.

'You're back,' he says, rushing towards me. 'Thank God. I was worried I would have to come and find you.'

'I'm fine,' I say, though I sound anything but. My eyes dart around the room. Why's he here? Surely he should be out by now? I know the easiest thing to do is ask him, but I can't bring myself to do that. Not when I'm certain that every word that's going to leave his mouth will be a lie.

'Frankie, we need to talk.' He moves forward as if he's about to hug me, and my body goes rigid. With a flash of pain on his face, he stops. God, he's such a good liar. It makes me sick. My hands clench at my side, and I swear that if I had a knife within reach, I would stab him with it, just so he could understand a fragment of the pain he's causing me. I trusted him. I trusted him and he's been playing me for a fool.

'You need to sit down. Please,' he says. His hands are outstretched, as if he's approaching a scared animal, and I'm about to tell him to drop the act, but before I can, he carries on. 'We need to talk about something.'

'No, no.' I shake my head. 'No, you don't get to do this. You don't get to tell me what I can and—'

'Please, Frankie. You need to listen. It's about Gloria.'

Her name is about the only thing that could stop the words from spilling from my lips.

'Gloria?'

My eyes lock onto his and no matter how much of a liar I know he is, no matter how freaking twisted he is, I swear the pain I see is real.

'I'm sorry, Frankie. I am,' he says.

54

My head is shaking back and forth. I can feel the skin of my cheeks slapping against my jawbones, but I can't stop the motion.

'She's dead,' he says, as if I didn't understand what his look was already conveying.

'Did you do this?' The tears choke my throat. 'Did you kill her?'

'What? What are you on about, Frankie? Of course I didn't.'

'You've never been there.'

'What?'

'When I've had my meetings with Dr B. You've never been in the same place as me.' The thought process that allowed me to realise that Duncan is Dr B is rolling from my lips. 'That's how I figured it out. That's how I know what you've done.'

His brow pinches into a frown.

'Frankie, I think you're in shock right now. We were talking about Gloria.'

I shake my head repeatedly as if I'm trying to jostle the pieces of a jigsaw around to make sense of the pattern.

'You know me. You'd know I'd refuse. It would give you the

perfect alibi. You said you'd stay with me, but you never did. Not once. You've never been there, and you knew all about my parents. You knew all about Professor Jarvis and Heidi because I told you... you... you...'

'Look, you're in shock. Please, just come and sit down.'

I don't want to let him touch me, but I don't have the strength to move or fight him off, and when he takes me by the hand, I let him lead me across to the room.

'I'm sorry, Frankie. I don't know what else to say.' He pauses to release a sigh. 'I got a telephone call about an hour ago from her father. I couldn't go to work without you knowing, but I didn't want to ring you. It didn't seem right, you finding out like that.'

'No. You're lying to me. You have to be lying to me. It's just another of your games.'

'I'm not playing any games, Frankie. I swear on your life.'

'Right now, that doesn't mean much.'

I'm sitting in the armchair and though I don't know when I moved, I'm grateful I did. I don't think my legs have it in them to keep me standing. If Gloria's dead, there's one obvious reason: Duncan killed her. He didn't like that we were in contact again. That we could get close again, and so he killed her to stop that happening.

'Her dad was going through the names in her phone, calling people to let them know.' He carries on talking as if I hadn't spoken. 'It took him a while to face it and I think he was working his way through people alphabetically. You know, that's why he got to me before you. I hope you don't mind, but I told him not to worry about ringing you too. I said I'd let you know, but I have his number if you want to call him?'

I don't reply. Gloria didn't mention her father much. I don't know what he looks like, but in my head, an image forms of an older, male version of Gloria. Curly, dark hair. Deep-set eyes. I swallow back the image as it forms. I can't think about her now. Or more accurately, I don't want to think about her now.

Somewhere deep in my stomach, I knew that was the case. The second I'd seen the police cars at the café, part of me knew she was gone and this time, she wouldn't be coming back. But I refused to accept it. How? That's what I want to know. How did he do it? He owes me an answer to that question, at least.

'How? What happened?' I say, finally holding his gaze. 'How did she die?'

Did you make it painful like you did for Rupert Fitzherbert? I think, but I don't add that part.

'She drowned in the bath. But I think drugs were involved too. I didn't ask too much. I got the sense that these last few months have been tough for her father. Everything was very detached. As you'd expect. It felt like he had a bit of script to go through. I guess that makes sense.'

For a moment, there's nothing I can say until the exact words I need form on my tongue.

'You're lying.' I hold his gaze, almost so he can see my sanity. 'This is just part of some sick game. It is. I know it is. Either that, or you're the one who killed her.'

I have to give it to him; he is a master of facial expressions. The look of disgust that forms on his face is entirely believable. Or would be if I didn't know what he was up to.

'Frankie, I would never hurt anybody. I don't know what to say to that, other than I think you need some help. I really do.'

I'm not listening any more. I won't have it. With a sharp inhale, I push myself onto my feet and move towards the bedroom.

'What are you doing?' Duncan says, so close behind me I can feel the heat of his breath.

'I'm packing a bag and I'm going to see her family. I'm going up for the funeral, and while I'm there, I'm going to find out exactly what happened.'

'Frankie, you need to listen,' he says as I grab a bag and empty out the contents, ready to refill it. 'Listen to me!'

He takes me by the wrist and swings me around to face him. His face is red, teeth bared.

'Let go of me. Now,' I hiss.

'Frankie, you don't understand.'

'Oh, I do.'

'No. No, you don't.' Duncan chews down on his bottom lip. It's like he can't meet my eye any more.

'I'm sorry, the funeral has already happened.'

'What? Why? I don't understand. It normally takes a couple of weeks, doesn't it? Two weeks, that's the average. I can't have missed it. I can't have missed her funeral.'

His grip on my arms has tightened and there's a new pale sheen to his cheeks. A single tear rolls down towards his chin.

'It was six months ago, Frankie. The funeral was six months ago. That was when she died.'

55

I don't understand. Nothing Duncan is saying is making sense. And it doesn't help that he's looking at me with an expression I can't read.

'That... that can't be right. I spoke to her... I spoke to her two weeks ago.'

His Adam's apple rises and falls several times before he speaks again.

'I know that you think you did,' he says eventually.

I feel my face frown before the weight of his words sink in.

'I *think* I did? What the hell is that meant to mean? I spoke to her on the phone twice and I arranged to meet her at the café. You know this. You know that when I got to the café, the police were there. The police were there and a woman of her description got taken away in an ambulance.' I can see it all so clearly in my head as I repeat the moments of that day. I can feel it. The fear in my stomach when I turned that corner. That can't all be a coincidence. I press my fingers against my temples, trying to stop the pounding beneath them. 'You know all of this. You helped me ring the hospitals, for fuck's sake!'

'I remember. I remember how upset you were, but...' His voice trails off.

'But?' What the hell can follow a but in a situation like this? 'This is you, Duncan. This is all you. You're doing this to me. Messing with my head. I need to speak to her father.'

'I think you need to calm down first. Please, you're getting yourself into a state. I don't think speaking to anyone the way you are is going to help anything.'

A state. That's what he wants to call it? He's acting like I'm losing the plot. Like I'm insane. When he's the one that's doing it all. I grit my teeth and try to steady my thoughts. I promised myself I wasn't going to do this. I wasn't going to stop thinking straight. I'm not crazy, he's just trying to make me believe that and I won't play his games.

'Whatever you think you're gaining from this, you're not,' I say, my gaze unblinking as I stare at him. 'I spoke to her. I was texting her. I can prove it. So you go tell anyone you want that I'm losing my mind, or that Gloria died six months ago, they won't believe you, because I have the truth. Just like I'll find out the truth about you and Rupert.'

'Rupert? Who's Rupert?'

Ignoring his feigned ignorance, I pull my phone out of my pocket, a burning satisfaction filling me. His reign of manipulation is about to come to an end.

It only takes a minute before my screen is filled with the messages Gloria and I have exchanged. The most recent are all from me, asking if she is okay. Mentioning the café. I keep going up and up until I reach some earlier ones.

> I miss you. I just want to know you're okay.
> Duncan and I move today.

I stop. I've gone too far back. This was the message I sent a year and a half ago, when we had finally left my parents' place. I scroll back down until I hit a strip of short messages about wanting to speak to her and the pin from the café.

Again, I've gone too far.

I check up again. But there's nothing. Didn't she respond? I'm sure she did? But all the messages are from me. There's nothing from her. The voice calls came from me. The map location. They're all sent by me. There's nothing from her. Not for months and months.

'I was never there when you spoke to her,' Duncan says quietly. 'You were always on your own, right?'

I nod, not because I want him to think I'm siding with his thoughts in any way, just because it's the truth.

'I was always on my own,' I whisper.

'I'm sorry, Frankie,' he says, now with both hands on my shoulders. 'But you didn't speak to her. You couldn't have. Gloria had already died. And I know it's not easy to hear, but I think it's time you admit you need to get some help.'

56

The silence is all-consuming. Sounds drift up from the road below – cars, laughter – but none of them can penetrate my thoughts.

I look at Duncan. There's so much pain and worry in his eyes, but is it real? I don't think so, but I'm starting to doubt my own thoughts.

'I need you to get out,' I say.

'What?' Duncan releases my shoulders to look at me.

'I don't know why you did this. I don't know what game you're playing, but it's over. You need to leave now.'

He steps towards me, but I flinch. Confusion clouds his face, as if he can't understand why I'm repulsed by him. But it's all part of an act that I'm no longer falling for.

'Frankie.' He stands with his hands open to me. 'I don't know what's happening right now, but I swear I have nothing to do with it. Other than relaying the message. Look at my phone. Ring Gloria's dad if that's what you need to do. But before you do, I need you to listen to something.'

'I've listened to you far too much,' I say, but he carries on anyway.

'I know this isn't what you want to hear, but I think... but I think you're unwell. I think it's stress or something else, but you're not well. Surely you can see that.'

I don't mean to laugh. But it's a reflex response. High-pitched and grating, it reverberates in the air.

'I'm unwell?' The laugh continues. 'You're joking, right? Oh my God, you're gaslighting me. That's what you've been doing for this entire relationship. You're the one pulling all these stunts. Who murdered Rupert.'

'Murdered... What the fuck, listen to yourself—'

'You're the one who's cheating on me—'

'I am not cheating on you.'

'I saw the photos, the receipts for the toll—'

'The toll that you paid for, Frankie!'

It's the second time he's shouted at me today, but before now, I don't think I've ever heard Duncan raise his voice. Not to me, or anyone. But it's his words, more than the tone, that cause me to stop.

'What are you on about?' I frown. 'I didn't pay for any toll.'

'It's there in your bank account. The payments. Mersey Toll. Not our joint account. Yours.'

I know that Duncan has access to all my passwords and account details. I thought it was the level of trust we shared. I didn't realise he would use it to gaslight me.

'What were you checking my account for? Were you hoping to siphon some more of my money before I kicked you out?'

His jaw twitches, but he manages to keep his voice restrained.

'I was just checking how much you'd got in your account. It wasn't right of me, I know that, but I was trying to figure out bills and stuff and working out how many lessons I needed in order to cover this new place. I thought if I could take some of that burden off you, it would help. So I checked last night, when you went to bed. I'm sorry, but I'm glad I did. I don't think I'd have realised how serious it was if I hadn't seen that.' He pauses, tears brimming his eyes, and as he blinks, several spill over. Hurriedly, he wipes them away. 'Frankie, you are the one who made those payments. You can see for yourself.' He hands me my phone and almost reflexively, I open up my banking app. Even when I've stopped scrolling, Duncan carries on speaking. 'It's there, isn't it? Two receipts for the Mersey toll came out of your account. And I was gigging when they were made. You can check that with Tommy or whoever you want, but there was no way I could've done that. Look, I don't know what's going on with you right now, but I promise I will help you through it, okay? Through it all. It's going to be all right.'

57

I try Gloria's father's number half a dozen times, and each time, the call rings out.

'Please, Frankie, we need to talk about this,' Duncan says as I finally give up and hurl my phone across the room.

'There's nothing to talk about. Not to you anyway,' I snap back.

Ignoring the fact that it's not even six yet, I pick my phone back up and take myself to bed. I don't care. I just need a place to shut off. To block out everything I've just learned.

I know it's Duncan who's doing this to me. After all, who else would have access to all my bank details? It's a great ploy. A way to cover up the cheating and simultaneously make it look like I'm losing the plot, but at the same time, I don't know what I'm supposed to do now. He has so much control. That's what this is proving to me. He has the power to manipulate me in a way that I never envisaged possible. Now it makes sense where the flowers came from too. He just acted like they weren't from him so that I'd start questioning things. Maybe he thought that by keeping me scared, he'd keep me complicit. He knows me. Knows my weaknesses. Know how to murder people and make it look like suicide. A new sickness forms as I realise that was what he probably did to Gloria too.

My mind whirrs. He's likely to have already predicted any rash or impulsive plans that I could make. Ways to stop me from kicking him out of the apartment or going to the police and telling them what he's done. I have to be smarter than that. I have to act slowly and consider every move or I'll end up like my mother. Killed by the hand of the person I loved and trusted. I don't think I'd ever truly considered it as a possibility before. Never honestly admitted to myself it could have been my father. There'd always been so much doubt, because I thought I knew him better than the police or the forensics or the damn vultures writing their newspaper articles. I believed I knew what type of person he was. Well, I thought I knew the type of person Duncan was too, and look where that's got me. At least I've got an advantage my mother didn't have. She didn't see what type of person my father was until it was too late and that gun went off. But I've seen Duncan's true colours now and when I'm done with him, he will never hurt me or anyone else again.

'I hate to do this,' Duncan says, opening the bedroom door and stepping inside. I don't know how long I've been in our room for, but outside the light's fading, so I'd guess an hour or so. 'I've got to go for a gig, but I don't mind staying if that's what you want me to do.'

I don't even bother replying. Instead, I roll over in the bed so I'm no longer facing him.

'Frankie, please, I just want to help you.'

'I'll make sure people know the truth,' I say as I stare at the blank wall in front of me. 'I don't know why you're doing this. This isn't protecting me. Gloria was never a threat to us. Rupert was never a threat. Whatever you think you've got planned, you won't manage to keep it hidden forever. I'll make sure of it.'

Five minutes later, the front door goes.

I know I need to use this time and leave. I need to get away from him, but where?

Heidi – that's my only possibility right now. I get up, grab my phone and try to ring her. The call goes straight to voicemail, so I fire off a message:

> Something's happened; I need to come to yours. I need to explain.

I check for a second to make sure it's gone through, then hastily grab the bag I was going to pack earlier. I don't know what I need. Nothing really. I'm sure Heidi has everything, but is her place really the best to go to? It's probably the first place Duncan would look, but at least I'll be protected there. She has her followers, her social media presence. Maybe that can be an advantage. Surely he wouldn't risk trying anything under the scrutiny of 100,000 pairs of eyes.

When the bag's packed with the basics, I pick up the phone again. Still, there's nothing. I try another message, like the first. This one doesn't go through. Is she away somewhere? Maybe somewhere with a bad connection. I can't wait; I just have to go anyway. Worst-case scenario, I'll book into a random hotel until she gets back.

I head into the living room and scan the area. There's nothing I need other than my laptop, which is already packed, my wallet and my card. For a second, I think about leaving my phone. It's got the location app on it that Duncan uses to see where I am – something I'd thought of as reassuring before, but of course it wasn't. It was manipulative. But maybe... maybe I need to leave it on for now. If I delete it, I won't know where he is either. At least this will give me a warning if he's coming after me.

Happy I've got everything, the last thing I need is my keys. I go to pick them up from the hook by the door, only to find they're not there. My pulse is soaring but I try to stay calm. I just need to think logically. Where did I put them? I wasn't expecting Duncan home, so that would've disrupted me. But where did I put them? I race through my mind, trying to remember the moment, but I'm sure I hung them up. I always hang them up.

With my breathing getting shallower and shallower, I consider my options. What do I need in this flat? Nothing really. I'm not going to come back, so what does it matter if I lock up or not? With my mind made up, I go to open the door, only it doesn't move. I push down on the handle a little harder this time and push it with all my weight. Still, there's nothing.

Duncan locked me in. He's fucking locked me in.

58

It's not just the front door. It's the balcony door too. There is no way for me to get out of this flat.

What the fuck? He's made me an actual prisoner. Not just in my mind, but actually a prisoner. I pick up my phone and hit dial.

He picks up immediately.

'I will ring the police,' I say the second he answers. 'I will ring the police, and you will go to jail for this. You will.'

'Look, it's for your own safety. I'm sorry. I promise. Look, I'm coming back home now. I shouldn't have done it. I was just worried, okay? You have to understand that, right? You have to understand that I'm worried. You think you've been talking to a person who is dead.'

'Who you killed.'

'Please, Frankie—'

I hear in his voice that wherever he is, people have started to look at him.

'I'll come home now. I will. I've already called somebody.'

'Somebody? Who do you mean, somebody?'

'Somebody to do an assessment.'

'Assessment? You mean on me?'

I don't need him to answer that. And whether for my sake or his, he doesn't.

'I'm sorry, but I think it's what you need right now. They're going to come by in the morning, okay? First thing. And it's important you be there. I'm not manipulating you. I'm not lying to you. I'm trying to help you, but if you're not there, Frankie, they will section you. If you bolt, they will section you.'

I cannot believe it. I cannot believe what I'm hearing. 'I'm going to call the police.'

'Then they'll just section you even faster. If you could stop and listen to yourself for one minute, you would see that.'

'Oh my God, I can't believe you're doing this to me.'

'*For* you, Frankie. I'm doing it *for* you. Please. Just... I'll be home in a little bit. Try to get some sleep, okay? Eat something. There's food in the fridge.' He pauses before speaking again. 'I know you don't believe me, but I really do love you.'

'You're right,' I say. 'I don't.' Then I hang up.

59

It's not just Duncan that's against me. My body is too. I know it's probably from lack of sleep last night, but the harder I try to stay awake, the heavier my eyelids become. When I hang up the phone, I originally have a plan of staying awake and overpowering him the second he opens the door. It's a shit plan, admittedly, but a plan nonetheless. But even sitting in the armchair causes the weight of my body to quadruple. My limbs feel so dense that I can't even stand up, and I know I won't win any battle like this. As I close my eyes, I promise myself it's just for fifteen minutes. A power nap. Only when I wake up, I'm back in a bed.

With a jerk, I sit upright, pulse racing. It takes me a second to recognise my surroundings as our new bedroom, although rather than relief, it's a sense of anger that fills me. I should've known that Duncan would carry me in here, but it's going to be the last time I let him touch me in any way. Just knowing he picked me up and had his hands around me causes the bile to sting the back of my throat. I can't do it. I can't be in this place with him any longer. And I'm not going to give him the chance to have me locked away, either. No, this ends today.

I'm still in the clothes I was wearing yesterday, and I'd rather stink than risk waking him up. So, dressed as I am, I creep out of the bedroom. Duncan is fast asleep on the armchair again. His head lolls to the side slightly as a gentle snore rolls off his lips. I go to close the bedroom door – hoping he'll assume I'm still inside when he wakes up – but as the hinges creak, he stirs and his snore stutters. I stop dead, my heart pounding. I can't afford to wake him, not until I've got a plan. I stay like that, listening to my heartbeat getting faster and faster until his breaths fall back into a steady rhythm. Even then, I stay where I am.

You have to move at some point, Frankie, I say to myself. *If you don't move now, you might never get the chance.*

The words finally provide the impetus I need to push myself from the doorway. As I move across the living area and spot his phone on the table, a thought strikes.

He should have changed his password, I think as I pick up his phone and delete the location app. At least he won't be able to follow me directly. That's something. A small sense of relief flutters with me, although as I go to put it down, another thought strikes. With one eye on Duncan, making sure that his snoring is steady and there's no chance of him waking up, I open his recently called list.

I scan down to the number he told me was Gloria's father. The number I tried ringing from his phone half a dozen times last night. I don't bother trying to ring it again now though; instead, I put it in my phone and take his keys from where they hang by the door. Evidence. Everything is evidence.

60

On the way to campus, I try to call the number from the phone. I must hit dial a dozen times, but each time, it rings out completely before it starts going to voicemail. I don't think it's her father's number, anyway. It's more likely Duncan got an extra phone so that he could ring himself and make it look like he'd had some long conversation.

He's smart, I'll give him that. But he's not smart enough to get away with this.

My aim is to find Heidi, tell her what's happened, then come up with a plan together. The first thing is to log all the evidence of things he's done to manipulate me before, going as far back as possible. The problem is, before this week, I never realised what he was up to, so it's going to require some serious memory power.

Given that it's Professor Jarvis's lecture first thing, I assume Heidi will be there. With everything that's happened, it's probably not a surprise I'm running late for it. Still, it's only just starting as I slip in at the back of the hall.

For a second, I think I'm in the wrong place as Dr Ribero

moves to the front of the podium, and while a few people fall silent, the general chatting continues until she clears her throat.

'Good morning, everyone. I'm afraid Professor Jarvis will not be able to attend lectures for the remainder of the semester, but do not worry. He has left the faculty all his notes and we will relay them to you. Now, we should get on.'

For a split second, the room is silent. Then it erupts. Talking starts from every direction and dozens of hands appear in the air, many of them not waiting for Dr Ribero to address them before they ask a question.

'Where has he gone? Why can't he come back?'

'Is he sick? What about our grades? Is it going to affect us having a change of lecturer halfway through the course?'

'What about the people in his seminar classes?'

'I'm afraid I don't have all the information just yet. There is going to be no leniency on grades, I'm afraid, and every class will be informed individually. Now, we've already lost several minutes of this class, and there's a lot Professor Jarvis has left us to get through. So, if you don't mind, let's begin the class and if you have any questions or issues, please email them to me after the session.'

Finally, the hall quietens down and Dr Ribero starts the lecture. She does a good enough job, but you can see that no one is really paying attention. Whispers are constantly skirting around the room, people scribbling notes on pieces of paper or typing on their laptops and twisting the screens around to show their neighbours. Curiosity is everywhere, and learning has taken second place to gossip. As much as I'd like to say I'm better than them, I want to know what has happened to Professor Jarvis too, although my concern is likely more genuine. I at least know him, to a small degree anyway.

The Student

> Is Ivor okay?

I fire off the message to Heidi, not caring that I'm in the middle of a class, but once again, it's not going through. Just like none of my messages last night did. What was previously a sense of mild annoyance has shifted to a far greater level of concern. Why would a message not go through to her? There's no chance she would go twelve hours with her phone off or out of charge. She has power bars and battery packs galore. Did Duncan get to her? Is that where he was last night? What did he do? He would have known she was my only place to go for support. Oh my God. That has to have been what he was doing.

The feeling of nausea causes me to bolt from the lecture.

In desperate need of fresh air, I head straight outside, but by the time I hit the lawn, I'm struggling to control my breathing. Something's happened to Heidi. I'm certain of it. Something's happened.

'I was hoping to see you.'

The relief washes through me in such a torrent, I lose my breath yet again as I look up and see Heidi standing in front of me. Yet, she doesn't look like Heidi. Her eyes are bloodshot, and her face is uncharacteristically blotchy, particularly around her nose, which looks as if it has been blown red raw. Her hair is unbrushed and there isn't a scrap of makeup on her; it's definitely not an image she'd put on Instagram. A new sense of sickness fills me as the worst-case scenarios run through my head.

'Heidi,' I say. 'What happened? Is Ivor okay?'

Rather than collapsing in tears, or wrapping her arms around me, as I expect her to do, Heidi's eyes narrow and her top lip curls upwards into a snarl. 'Don't you dare lie to me, you bitch. I know it was you. I know you did this, and I'm going to make you pay.'

61

Several people have stopped, or slowed their pace, clearly wanting to know what's going on. And they're not the only ones.

'Sorry?' I say, trying to make sense of Heidi's outburst. 'I don't know what you're talking about. What happened to Ivor?'

Daggers blaze in her eyes, and they're all aimed directly at me. 'You just couldn't deal with it, could you? You just couldn't deal with him choosing me.'

'Sorry?'

'I saw the way you were looking at him outside the lecture hall. You thought that little moment would be enough for you to take him from me. Well, you're wrong. It didn't work. And neither will this stunt. I promise you that.'

The confusion I was feeling only moments ago is fading, and a low simmering anger is taking its place.

'You mean when he told me someone we know had died? Look, Heidi, I don't know what the hell you're on about right now, but whatever has happened, I'm not responsible. Duncan—'

She tips her head back and laughs. It's nasal and grating and sounds like nails on a chalkboard.

'You're crazy, you know that? Ivor might get permanently suspended for this. Do you have any idea what you've done? Six months. For six months, we were perfectly happy, and then the week after you find out, someone suddenly tells the university. You can't tell me that's a coincidence.'

'I haven't done anything.' I spit my words at her as loud as I can without outright shouting. 'Whatever has happened, whatever you think I've done, I can promise you, I'm not responsible.'

It's like my words are bouncing straight off her. Like she doesn't even hear them.

'I will make sure you pay for this. You understand? I will make sure you get everything you deserve. I don't care how tragic your past is; you don't get to pull stunts like this. Not to people who are supposed to be your friends. But I guess I understand why you don't have any of those now.' She scoffs a little, as if what she said was actually humorous. 'Now, if you don't mind, I need to try and put my boyfriend's life back together, after you just ruined it.'

With that, she turns around and marches off towards the main road.

It's only when she's gone that I realise just how much of a crowd her little scene brought in.

'It's over,' I say, turning around and trying to look into people's eyes as I do. 'Show's over. You can go about your day now.'

The whispering continues, but the crowd disperses pretty quickly. Mostly outside, but one or two head back upstairs towards the lecture halls. That's where I should be going too, only my feet don't want to move.

'So that didn't sound like the most pleasant conversation.' I turn around to find myself face to face with Will, the PhD student who can normally be found ferrying Professor Jarvis's coffees around. 'You okay?'

A sniff is the only immediate response I can offer.

'Let's just say I've had better days.'

He nods, the way people always do when they're not sure how they're supposed to respond.

'I'm heading down to the coffee shop to grab a drink if you want to get out of here for a bit and need some company?'

It's a sweet offer, and I genuinely consider it. I might not know him, but I get the impression he's not the type of person to enjoy vacuous gossip, but then, I don't really have it in me to talk to anyone right now.

'I should get to my lectures,' I say instead. My scholarship is currently the only thing I have left. I won't let Duncan take that from me too.

'Okay, well, I'm here if you need someone to talk to.'

I don't even bother saying thank you as I turn around and walk back into the building.

62

I head to the library, but I don't know what it is I intend on doing. My head is a mess. Hundreds of conflicting emotions and thoughts all fighting for space in my mind. All I can do is close my eyes and try to hush them.

Heidi can't seriously think I'm responsible for telling the university about her relationship with Professor Jarvis. Surely she knows me better than that, but then, why would she? I thought I knew Duncan better than anyone and I never would have dreamt he could do this.

As if he knows that I'm thinking about him, a message pings through on my phone.

> I need to know you're safe. Please don't do anything silly. We'll get you the help you need. I promise. I'm not mad. I love you.

'Fucking bastard.'

It's the way he's so desperate to convince me he's on my side – it should be laughable, only right now, I'm on the verge of tears. I thought I had dealt with everything life could throw at me, that nothing would be able to break me again, but he's doing his best and if I don't get away from him for good, he might just succeed. Why? That's the question I need an answer to. Why would he do this to me? It can't be to hurt me. He's had too many opportunities for that in the past, so it has to be because he wants to protect me. Maybe he thinks me doubting my sanity will stop me ever leaving him? Surely not. I shake the questions away. The why doesn't matter. What I need now is to find a place I can go where he won't look for me. Somewhere safe. A women's refuge, perhaps? A glimmer of hope helps me battle down the tears. Yes, that could work. I open up the browser on my phone and find the page from where I googled Duncan's dead brother is still open. The fact he didn't lie about that isn't any great source of comfort. Not really. But it triggers another thought. Why did I just take his word that Gloria had died? Especially now I know the number he's given me doesn't go through? And if Gloria is still alive, she will help me put Duncan behind bars where he belongs.

I open up a search bar and begin to type: *death, Gloria Noland*. It can't be that common a name, can it?

With my pulse pounding against my eardrums and a rush of adrenaline coursing through my veins, I close my eyes, ready to hit the enter button. *Please show nothing. Please be nothing.* I say the words on repeat in my mind like a mantra. Even when I tap the keyboard, I keep my eyes closed for a moment longer.

When I finally open them, a stifled gasp catches in my throat. The first entry is from the *York Echo*. I don't need to click on the link to see what it says.

Gloria Noland, of Halifax, died fourth of January.

Gloria is dead, so who the hell was I talking to?

63

I slump in the back of my chair, a strange numbness filling my body. Gloria is dead. I didn't know it, but Gloria is dead, and yet I would have bet my life that I had spoken to her. I can still hear that panic that rose the pitch of her words. The inflections caused by breathing and fear. I would have bet my life I had spoken to her, just like I would bet my life Duncan has been lying to me. So what the hell does that mean? There's one obvious answer. One that he's been trying to tell me since he first noticed it. I'm going crazy. I'm going crazy. If I can make up something like speaking to a dead person, then of course I could've paid that damn toll for Duncan, or told the university about Heidi and Rupert. Clearly, I don't know what I'm capable of. I'm sick.

Another thought forms, and it turns my veins to ice. Maybe I'm not the first person in my family to go insane.

My throat tightens. For so many years, I had been convinced my father was innocent. Even when the police sat me down and told me there were no other suspects, that the case was cut and dry, that this was a textbook murder-suicide between loved ones.

Even then, I refused to believe that my father, whom I loved and adored and believed I knew, would do something like that. But over the last twenty-four hours, my mind has shifted. I believed Duncan was manipulating me and that my mother, like me, had remained oblivious to this other side of her partner until it was too late. But maybe I was wrong to think I was like my mother in the situation. Maybe whatever is going on with me happened to my father too. Maybe it's some hereditary sickness that we can't escape. Maybe I'm the one with the potential to become a killer.

Tears streak down my cheeks. I need help. I need somebody to put me away somewhere where I can't be a risk to myself or anyone else. It's just like Duncan said. Whatever he's sorted, wherever he's found, I need to go. I can see that now.

I pick up my phone and hit dial.

'Frankie, thank God. Are you okay?' Duncan's voice is full of compassion. That's all it was ever full of – not lies. Compassion. I shake my head, only to realise he can't see me.

'No, I don't think I am.'

'What's happened? Has something happened?' I hear the panic rise.

'She died… she died six months ago…'

There's silence. 'I know… I know she did.'

'And… and…' For a split second, I consider telling him about Heidi, only to stop myself. It's not going to change anything. 'Can you come and get me? I think… I think I need help.'

'Just stay where you are, okay? I'm over on the other side of town at Tommy's. It'll take me about forty minutes, but stay where you are, okay?'

'Okay.'

'Are you at the library?' His voice is airy, like he's rushing around as he speaks to me. He probably is.

'Yes. In the library in the English building.'

'Well, just stay where you are. Don't move. I'm coming to get you, okay? I'm coming to get you, and I love you, Frankie. You know that, right? I love you, it's gonna be fine.'

I hang up the phone without replying. I'm not sure anything will ever be fine again.

64

I caused him so much shit. That's what I keep thinking as I sit here, Duncan's words echoing in my head. I put him through hell. I acted like he was dangerous. Manipulating me. And the entire time, he was only trying to help. Trying to be the best possible boyfriend he could be.

It's gonna be fine. That's what he said, but it won't be. I don't know much, but I know that. What could my future possibly be now? Duncan will want to stay with me through this. He'll want to get me through it, but that's not fair on him – it's just not – so I'm going to have to make him leave. I could make out that I still believe he's lying and that I don't trust him, but I don't think that would work. Maybe I could convince him I don't love him any more. Or that I never did. I don't know how I'm going to do it, exactly, but I know I can't be with him. I can't do this course either. This degree that I fought tooth and nail to get onto. Not unless they allow distance learning from whatever ward they're going to lock me away in. Which means this will probably be my last day here.

As I look around me, I notice people standing up, milling

The Student

about, and as I check the time, I realise my second lecture's about to start. There feels little point going, other than it being my last chance to do so. As I watch several other people from my course leaving, a pang of jealousy hits. They don't know how lucky they are.

With that feeling firmly in my gut, I stand up. I'll just do forty minutes. Half an hour even. Duncan will text me when he gets here. And I'd prefer my last memories at this place were positive, rather than being of me sitting here alone with my insanity.

As I walk into the back of the lecture hall, several heads turn to look in my direction. Probably because of the argument I had with Heidi. No doubt the rumours have already spread throughout the faculty, but I don't care. People can call me crazy all they want. It doesn't hurt when it's true. I take a seat at the back, open my computer and wait for the class to start. It's a lecture on narrative voice. It used to be one of my favourites, and I consistently came out with incredible grades. But maybe losing your mind allows you to tap into something other writers can't. I'm probably clutching at straws, but who knows, maybe if I get the help I need, then at some point later down the line, I can turn this into a best-selling novel. There's got to be some advantage to going crazy, hasn't there?

It's hard to focus, but I try. The title for the session is already on the whiteboard and I write it at the top of a blank page in my notebook before underlining it several times, like that's going to make a difference. I'm about to write the date too just so there's something else filling the empty space, but before I can, Dr Ribero appears at the front of the hall. For the second time today, she's standing in front of a class she doesn't take and staring straight into the rows of students.

It's like déjà vu. It's clear from the way she shifts her gaze about that she doesn't know who she's looking for, but her voice is clear and crisp.

'Sorry for the interruption,' she starts, and somehow, I already know what she's going to say next.

'I need Francesca Crawford to come to my office,' she says. 'Now.'

65

Three weeks ago, I'd never had my name called out during a lecture. Eighteen months of studying in the same place, and only one person knew who I was. Now all that's changed.

As I slowly rise to my feet, it feels like everyone in the room turns to look at me and there's nothing I can do to stop my cheeks from colouring.

Why would Dr Ribero want to see me? Is it something to do with Professor Jarvis? Does she, like Heidi, think I'm responsible for telling the university about the affair? What if she's great friends with Professor Jarvis and has come to accuse me? Shit, is she the one I told? Maybe I did and I've already forgotten.

Whatever the reason, I need to be put out of my misery. Yet as I follow her out of the hall, she doesn't even bother turning to look at me.

'We will speak in my office,' she says when we are part way down the staircase. 'The others are waiting for us there.'

'The others?'

She doesn't reply.

By the time we've made it to the bottom of the stairs, my hands are clenched so hard, I'm certain my nails have pierced the skin. Dr Ribero has barely said two words to me, but there's no doubt in my mind that whatever she wants to see me about isn't good. There's such a frostiness radiating from her body that I'm surprised she's not turning the world to ice as she walks.

Her office is a floor above Professor Jarvis's and as I cast my eyes down his corridor, I can't help but wonder how things would have panned out differently if I hadn't opened his office door that day. If only I hadn't found out about him and Heidi. It wouldn't change my state of mind. I know that. But at least I'd still have Heidi as a friend. Someone to help me through it. Not that she's ever been much good at listening to other people's issues.

When we reach her office, Dr Ribero opens her door and holds it ajar for me to walk through. Just like she said, she's not the only one. There are two other members of staff there. Dr Ward and Dr Krishnan. Dr Ward only runs seminars and masters lectures, while Dr Krishnan ran a module on perspective in the second term last year. Both of them are typically sour faced, but right now, they look like they've been on a steady diet of lemons for months. They are sitting on the same side of the desk as Dr Ribero's chair, making this look remarkably like an interview. Only I didn't apply for anything. Not that I know of.

'Take a seat,' Dr Ribero said. 'I assume you know why you are here?'

'No,' I say. 'Does this have anything to do with Professor Jarvis?'

Her nostrils flatten with a sharp sniff.

'No. It does not. The incident with Professor Jarvis is extremely upsetting, and exceptionally unprofessional, but not what we are here to discuss. We are here to discuss the fact that you handed in a piece of work that was not your work. That you handed in a poem, written by someone else, and tried to pass it off as your own. That, Ms Crawford, is a serious issue.'

66

All the lecturers' eyes are on me, unwavering, unblinking. But it's Dr Ribero who I can't take my attention away from. I'm sure I must have misheard her.

'Sorry?' I say. 'What are you saying I did?'

'Plagiarised. Copied. Cheated. The poem that you submitted to me as your final assessment is almost identical to one submitted by a student three years ago.'

I shake my head, trying to make sense of what I'm hearing.

'No, no, you're mistaken. I didn't... I wouldn't... I... I'm on a scholarship.'

Of all the things I'm struggling to believe I've done, this is the hardest one to swallow.

'Which is what makes your actions even more upsetting.' Dr Krishnan speaks up for the first time. He tuts before he continues. 'To think that the university would trust you with such a gift and you would abuse it in such a manner. That you would assume we wouldn't find out—'

'No, that's not what happened. I didn't. I swear.' My heart is hammering so fast, I think I'm going to pass out. 'I wrote that poem. I wrote it. I wrote so many drafts of so many poems. I swear, if there is any sort of passing resemblance between my work and another—'

'It is no passing resemblance.' Dr Ribero takes charge again. 'I would say there are only a dozen different words in the entire piece. The themes, the nuance, the measures, and cadence – they are all identical.'

It feels as though the ground has been knocked out beneath me. My friendship, my relationship, my future. I've destroyed them all and my broken mind won't even let me remember doing it. How can that be? How can I vividly recall talking to a person who's dead, but not remember paying for a toll or telling the university about my best friend's affair or submitting a piece of work that isn't mine? Where have those memories gone? Surely they must be in my head somewhere, but how can I get them out? And how can I get rid of the ones that aren't real? Is this what my father felt like? This insanity. This doubting his own actions. Maybe if he'd survived, he wouldn't even have remembered pointing the gun at my mum and pulling the trigger. I don't know if that's a consolation or not, but I need to stop this before I ruin someone else's life.

'Can I see the poem you're saying I copied? Please,' I whisper to Dr Ribero, hoping that seeing the poem might jolt a memory or two.

'Be my guest. We have printed it for you, and next to it, you will see the work you submitted as your own. I'm sure you will see the issue.'

Without another word, she slides a piece of paper across the desk towards me. I reach out and pick it up. Just like she said, she has printed the two poems side by side, landscape on the paper, and even without reading a word, I can see the similarities in the line lengths, the black and white patterns that occur in the spaces of the words. They are definitely similar, but as I read through the words, a rush of relief floods through me.

'Which one am I meant to have written?'

The scoff that comes from Dr Krishnan is enough to send him into a coughing fit, while Dr Ribero continues to stare at me.

'Surely you see that this is a major issue if you can't even tell which one is your own.'

'No, it's not that,' I say before I stop. How do I make them understand that I'm losing my mind? That I'm sick and I'm not just pretending to be ignorant?

'This is not looking good for you, Ms Crawford. If you can't even tell us about what work you supposedly did write...'

She lets the rest of her sentence drift into the ether, and the three lecturers exchange a look.

The disappointment is sharp. There's nothing in either poem that sparks the slightest bit of recollection. They are good, though. Probably better than I would have written. Is that why I submitted them? Because I thought I would get a better grade? It makes sense.

'Can I see the email it came from?' I ask, almost pleading. 'Maybe there's something written in there that'll... that will help.' Help? I'm not even sure what that word means any more. Maybe it'll add further proof to my belief that I'm going insane, or I'll have written a clue in the message. Something to draw the memories out of me. I'm starting to doubt that'll happen, though. It feels like parts of my brain have been vaulted off and I'm no longer allowed access.

At this, Dr Ribero arches an eyebrow, but as far as I'm concerned, it's an incredibly valid request, and thankfully, rather than reply, she opens up her laptop and taps a couple of times on the keyboard.

The heading is exactly as it should have been:

Assignment Three

'Ms Crawford, would you like to open up the attachments to this email for me, please?'

My stomach is a ball of knots, wanting to wrap around my intestines, but I breathe in as deeply as I can. I have not done this. Neither of those poems are mine, and when I open up these attachments, they'll all see that.

Trying to steady the tremble in my hand, I scroll down to the bottom, click on the icon for the attachment at the bottom of the page, but before it opens, I notice something. Something that causes my heart to somersault.

67

'That's not my email,' I say, feeling the surge of adrenaline and relief course through me.

'Sorry?' Dr Krishnan is once again taking a role. 'Francesca Crawford, that is you, isn't it?'

'Yes, yes, but there's a dot between the words. "Francesca.Crawford" – that's not my email. I don't have a dot. It's all one word. Straight through.'

Dr Ribero presses her lips tightly together before she speaks. 'Francesca, this is a university email. I can assure you I don't have somebody else on the register with the same name as you. I actually checked that today, just half an hour ago before I came to collect you.'

'I understand that,' I say, trying to keep my voice measured. 'I understand you don't have another person of that name here, but that is not my email address. Please, can you just check for me? Search again for the assignment. Search for Francesca Crawford without the dot in the email address.'

'This seems like a very elaborate waste of our time,' Dr Krishnan says. 'We have the evidence here in front of us.'

'You have the wrong evidence. Please. Somebody is setting me up.' Saying those words causes the air to rush into my lungs. *Somebody is setting me up.* Someone who wants me to think I'm going insane. 'Just search for the assignment – the submission for that. Please can you do that?'

Dr Ribero chews down on her bottom lip, and for a moment, I'm terrified she's going to dismiss me, but she nods. 'Give me a moment.'

Of all the lecturers for this to happen with, why did it have to be the one who is completely inept with technology? And how does she even cope in the real world? How does she pay her bills and order things online when she can't even connect a computer to the same projector she's been using for the last ten years? Of course, I can't say any of this. I have to keep it all in.

My fears and frustration suffocate me as the panic continues to rise. What the hell could she be doing that's taking her so long? I swear there should be some kind of rule, a minimum competency that lecturers should have to reach to be allowed to work with students. All I want to do is grab the laptop from her and swing it around so that I can read it myself, but obviously, I don't. I just sit there, listening.

'Hmm.' The sound causes my pulse to spike. 'It would appear that you are right. This is very strange.'

'I'm sure it's just an admin issue, you know, with ICT always changing servers and nonsense like that,' Dr Krishnan says, but Dr Ribero shoots him a look from which he shrinks back in his seat.

'I will admit this is interesting,' she says. 'Your first assignment did come from a different email address.'

'And this one too. I sent another. One that's not the poem you showed me. Can you check? Please?'

Another two minutes of torturous tapping follows, but she shakes her head.

'No, this is the only one I've got.'

It's not ideal, but at least she can see that something's not right here.

'Francesca...' Dr Ribero steeples her hands and rests her chin on her fingers. 'Can you think of anybody who would want to do this to you, who would deliberately try to sabotage your chances at the university?'

'Can I...' Her question causes a rush of air that forces the oxygen from my lungs. Though it takes me a moment to realise why. She believes me. She believes that something is happening to me – that someone is doing something to me.

'No, I don't know why they're doing it, but there have been other things.'

'Other things?'

How can I explain what has happened without them thinking I'm bonkers? Saying I spoke to someone who's been dead six months is the plot of a film, not the thing you say to make an academic believe you're telling the truth.

'Personal things,' I settle on. 'I think somebody is trying to ruin me. My chances here. My relationships.'

Her eyebrows rise simultaneously this time, high enough to reach her hairline.

'That is a serious accusation, Miss Crawford, but I will agree we need to look into this,' she says. 'This issue is not closed. We will be talking to you soon and if I find out who is behind this, you will be informed.'

'Thank you. Thank you.'

'You should go now. And take care, Francesca.'

I nod, my jaw clamped together.

'I will. I really will.'

68

What the fuck just happened? I feel like so many things just took place in the space of five minutes, my brain can't make sense of them all. I've not been kicked out of the university – that's something – but it's more... it's more than that. Of course it is. Somebody tried to pass an email off as me. Somebody created an email address to look like mine and Dr Ribero saw it. She saw it for what it was: somebody trying to harm me, to cause me pain. So maybe I'm not going crazy... maybe...

I press my fingers into my temples. There are still too many dots for me to see the big picture yet, but at least I can start to join them together, can't I?

'Think, Francesca, think.'

I don't care that I'm standing outside in a corridor, talking to myself. I'd sing naked wearing a one-man band costume if it meant I could get to the bottom of this.

Where are the dots? That's what I need to start with. I need to find all the dots and then I can start to join them.

It was an email, a university email. There's another jolt upwards in my pulse. That matters. Of course it does. It was set up on the university server, so not just anybody could do that, right? It would have to be somebody close to the university. Somebody in power. My head is starting to throb, but I'm getting close. I know I am. I can't stop now. What other dots do I have?

Dr B. Of course, all of this is linked to Dr B. Whatever he said, it wasn't a coincidence he sent me that photo of Duncan, just like it wasn't a coincidence that Rupert Fitzherbert died in the exact way he'd had me describe. I also know that he's male. It was a man's voice that spoke to me. So what man links the university to Dr B? Other than Rupert, who is now dead.

The thought lands like a hammer to the gut. The only person is Professor Jarvis. Professor Jarvis is behind it all. Framing himself was meant to be the perfect way to throw me off the scent before I was hauled into Dr Ribero's office. But it hasn't worked. I might not know why he's behind it, but I know he is.

A memory stirs in my mind. One that makes my throat turn bone dry and my hands start to tremble. One of the murders Dr B made me write was about an influencer. A young woman on social media who died from carbon monoxide poisoning so it looked like an accident and no one ever suspected foul play. Just like when Rupert killed himself. Who would be better placed to tamper with Heidi's boiler than the man she thinks she's in a relationship with?

Heidi is in serious danger.

69

Fear grips my stomach. My phone calls aren't going through, and why would they? Of course she's blocked me. He's convinced her I'm behind all this. He's trying to segregate us from one another's life. Maybe he's doing the same thing to her. Slowly making her think she's going insane. So many dots join at once, I have to close my eyes to stop them from overwhelming me. Maybe he even signed her up as a ghost-writer too. It would make sense why he was so insistent that I signed that NDA. It was so we wouldn't talk to one another about the project. So we wouldn't discover he was pulling this wool over our eyes all along.

'Shit, Heidi,' I say as I check the time on my watch. It's almost an hour since I saw her. Almost an hour ago since she said she was going to 'put his life back together'. He could've done anything in that time. So what do I do? I can't go to the police. I can already see how that will go down. There's nothing I can tell them that'll make them take me seriously. They already ruled Rupert's death as a suicide, and why would they care that somebody created an email address and submitted work pretending that they were me? That's hardly big police work. As for Gloria, I don't know how he pulled that off yet, but I will get there.

I don't know what to do, but I know I can't do nothing.

'Now, what did I say about you looking stressed again?'

I spin around to find myself face to face with the same PhD student who asked me out for a drink before.

'Does now look like a good time to hit on me?' I snap.

'I wasn't. I... Right, sorry, I should...' His cheeks turn fluorescent pink and I know I should probably apologise, but when he starts to walk away, a different thought strikes.

'You work with Professor Jarvis, don't you?' I say. 'Do you know where he lives?'

As he turns back, his eyebrows knit together. 'You need to reach Professor Jarvis? You know he's not allowed on campus. That he won't be assessing—'

'I need to speak to him. I need to see him.' My voice doesn't sound like mine. It's shrill and sharp and under any other circumstance, I'd start again, but I don't have time for that now. I just add one slight addition to my request. 'Please.'

'I believe he has been keeping his phone off a lot of the time. Understandably,' he says. 'I think he wants some privacy.'

'Do you know where he lives?' I ask again, realising he hasn't yet answered my initial question.

'I do, but...'

'But?'

'But I can't really give out his address to students. Data protection, you know?'

'For fuck's sake. Someone's life is in danger here!'

I don't mean to yell at him. He's actually being decent by protecting Jarvis. But I need a break. I need some way to get to him. To get to him before he hurts Heidi.

I go to walk away when he speaks again.

'I probably shouldn't say this to you, but I've actually got to head there now. I was on my way to see him.'

'What?'

He offers a quick shrug. 'The faculty has asked me to go collect his keys. They forgot to do it earlier. And I have one to his house too, for dropping off essays and things. I need to go, give that back.'

'You're going to his house,' I say. 'You're going now?'

He nods. 'I guess you can come with me? It sounds kind of serious.'

The relief is so great, I almost drop to my knees, but I don't. Somehow, I manage to stay standing.

'Thank you. Thank you. You have no idea how important this is.'

'It's okay, I kind of got that. My name's Will, by the way. Although some people call me Billy. Either's fine.'

70

Will leads the way as we walk on the pavement, away from the university. All the time, I have my phone in my hand, constantly checking, although what for, I'm not sure. Maybe that Heidi will suddenly come to her senses and ring me. It's wishful thinking but I can hope.

It's only when Duncan sends me a message saying he's been delayed by traffic that I remember I was meant to wait for him.

'Crap.'

I can't slow down or wait for him to get here. Every minute could be the difference between Heidi's life and death, and so, while still trying to weave my way through the crowd, I type a quick message.

> Think I know what's going on. Not at uni.

My message turns to read immediately, and only two seconds later, his name flashes up on my screen.

'Fuck,' I mutter.

Duncan still thinks I'm insane, meaning my text has probably sent him into panic overdrive, but I can't deal with it right now. I need to get Heidi out of there safely. Dr B – Professor Jarvis, whatever his name is – has already shown they're happy to throw Duncan under the bus. The last thing I need is for him to do that literally. I switch my phone onto silent, pull my rucksack off my back, and put it in one of the zip pockets. Then I return the bag to my back again, all without breaking stride.

'So I guess it must be serious if you need to speak to Ivor this urgently,' Will says, pulling me out of my thoughts. 'Do you wanna talk about it? Maybe I can help.'

'Trust me, you can't. It's fine, it's just… it's complicated.'

He looks away from me and hums, ever so slightly. The noise prickles my skin.

'It's not what you're thinking,' I say sharply. 'I'm not having an affair with him. That's not something I would do. Besides, I'm in a relationship.'

Once again, his cheeks turn pink. It's a state I can empathise with. I'm a blusher too and hate it when it happens to me, but right now, I've got bigger issues.

His voice crackles slightly before he carries on. 'Just so you know, I wasn't trying to be weird and hitting on you. I just thought… you know…'

'It's okay, don't worry.' My guilt intensifies.

There's no doubt that I'm putting Will in a seriously awkward position, but I can't focus on that now. The fact is he's doing a good deed, whether he knows that or not.

The pace is far quicker than I thought it would be, and more than once, I almost lose him amongst the people crowding on the pavement. But I guess a fast pace is good. The sooner I get to Professor Jarvis's house, the better.

'How far is it?' I say when we are forced to wait for the traffic to stop so we can cross a road.

He shrugs. 'Five more minutes.'

'Right.'

'So I take it you don't live close?' he says.

I shake my head. 'Not really. About twenty minutes from campus,' I tell him. 'Though in the opposite direction.'

'There are some nice areas around. So, it won't be long until you finish your second year. Have you thought about what your plans are after next year? Masters, I take it?'

'I don't know,' I say truthfully.

'Well, you've definitely got talent. I can tell that from what I read. I really enjoyed your assignments.'

'Thank you.'

Despite the compliments, I'm done with this. I don't have the mental capacity. It feels like we've been walking for a lot more than five minutes and this is definitely not the type of area I expected Professor Jarvis to live in. Not at all. But then, if you splash out large quantities of cash to manipulate people under the guise of getting them to ghost-write for you, I guess it doesn't leave a lot of money for rent.

'How much further did you say it is?' I ask.

'Two minutes, max. It'll probably be best if I go in first, you know. See what kind of state he's in. Whether he's up to talking. You know.'

'Right, of course. Yes.'

I'm being polite purely to appease Will. The second I see Professor Jarvis, I am going to wrap my hands around his throat until he explains what the fuck he's been doing. Either that or until I strangle him. Right now, I'll take either.

I'm still envisioning how the hell this is going to go down when Will stops.

'Okay, so this is it. We're here.'

71

We are standing outside a large, terraced house with bay windows and a metal railing above the basement. From the row of buzzers on the wall, it's obviously been broken up into flats, and I'm not convinced all of them are occupied. The first floor doesn't have any curtains, which can't be what you'd want in a place where you are completely overlooked, and the steps are covered in months' worth of fliers and takeaway menus.

'Okay, I'll just go down and check on him, all right?' Will says. 'I've got a couple of faculty messages to pass on. Are you okay to wait out here for a minute?'

'Sure,' I say, while simultaneously accepting that I'm going to ignore everything Will just said.

Waiting is the worst idea possible. The moment that door opens, I'm going down into the flat and demanding answers. Or at least getting Heidi out of there.

'Okay, well…' He smiles. 'I'll just be a second.'

He walks down the steps to the basement and out of my view. I'm in a catch twenty-two. I could move so that I could see him, but then there's a good chance Professor Jarvis would be able to see me too and I don't want that to happen. If it does, I won't get into that flat and he might hurt Heidi just to spite me. So I have to stay hidden. Just for the moment. I don't know whether Will hits a buzzer or knocks on the door, but his voice rings through incredibly clearly. Deliberately, perhaps? To let me in on the conversation? My gratitude swells. Thank God I found him. That's all I can think right now.

'Professor Jarvis?' Will's voice chimes. 'It's Will here. I've just come to bring your keys. Is that all right?'

He pauses. I can't hear a response, but Will obviously can.

'Okay, well, I've got some papers. Yes, a cup of tea would be great, thank you,' he says. A moment later, I hear the click of a heavy lock, immediately followed by the grating sound of an old door opening.

My heart leaps. I need to go now, before the door shuts. Before Professor Jarvis has a chance to get away from me. I don't pause for breath as I bolt down the stairs. The door is still slightly ajar, and that's all I need. With a pounding pulse, I push it open and step inside, but I'm immediately disorientated. Everything is dark. Every curtain drawn, blacked out, and the only real light is coming from the door. I turn around, trying to get my bearings.

A second later, it slams behind me, before clicking closed.

'Now, how did I know you weren't going to wait?'

72

'Don't worry, Frankie, I'm not really that mad.' Will's voice is soft. Low. 'It's actually quite funny. The fact that I knew you'd do that. Don't you think? Don't you think it's funny that I knew what you'd do?'

He's standing so close, that even in the low light, I can see the slanted smile which curls up one corner of his mouth as his tongue flickers out repeatedly to lick his bottom lip. His eyes are locked on me, glinting and yet unblinking. He looks insane.

'Will?' I try to keep my voice steady, though every inch of my body is shaking. I don't dare look away from him, but at the same time, I'm desperate to scour my surroundings and see if there's a way out of this. 'I don't know what's going on right now, but you don't have to do this. Whatever it is, you don't have to do. I'll leave now. I'll leave now and forget any of it ever happened. You have my word. I won't even tell the university. I promise. If you let me go now, I swear I won't tell anyone.'

'You don't need to sound afraid, Frankie. It'll all make sense soon.'

My throat is so dry, I can't even swallow, but I focus on my hands. On stretching my arms out and trying to understand my surroundings. Maybe if I can feel the door, I can figure a way out? I've got to do something.

'If I don't need to be afraid, then perhaps you can turn the lights on and prove that to me?' I say. I try to sound reasonable. To not yell and scream and thrash out the way I want to do. Something in my head is telling me that if I can just keep the situation calm, then maybe I can get out of it alive. I have to get out of it alive.

'I will. I just need a minute. That's all. Sorry. Sorry it had to start like this.'

I can tell from the way the sound shifts that he's moving. I spin in a circle, trying to catch something – a shadow, a glimmer of light, some indication of where he is – but there's nothing. The darkness is stopping me from thinking straight.

'Please, Will, whatever this is, just turn on the light. That's all I'm asking. Turn on the light so we can talk about it.'

'You're right. We do have a lot to talk about. You should cover your eyes now, before I turn them on. You'll need to give them a moment to adjust.'

I hear him move again. Hear the thud of his hand against the wall. That's where the door is, then. The way out. I try to get my bearings, but it's nearly impossible. I'm in no doubt that wherever he's brought me, it isn't Professor Jarvis's house. But what the hell have I done to Will that would make him do this to me? I rejected his offer of coffee that time – is that it? Did I unknowingly reject the offer of a psychopath? It's sure as hell starting to feel that way.

'I'm turning it on now. Have you shut your eyes?'

There's not a chance in hell I'm doing that, and he's stupid if he's even suggesting it in earnest, but perhaps that's something I can use.

'Sure, of course,' I say.

A millisecond later, the light switches on. It's blinding and my pupils respond reflexively, trying to block everything out. For a second, all I can see are blurry images. I have no choice but to squeeze my eyes closed and wait for the colour blotches that have seared onto my retina to fade.

'I told you, you needed to close your eyes,' Will says, his voice so close, I can feel his breath on my cheek. 'That was silly of you. I was only trying to keep you safe.'

I sweep out to hit him, only to strike empty air, but it won't happen again. My eyes have already readjusted, and after a couple of blinks, I can see clearly. My throat clamps shut.

It's a studio flat, though it's bigger than some I've come across. There's a television, a desk and a chair, along with the bed and bedside table, but it's not the furniture that holds my attention. It's not even Will himself. It's the walls. Walls that are covered in pictures. Most of them are small, family photos by the looks of things, but I gloss over most of them. It's the large one, directly above the desk, that holds my attention the most, and that's because I've seen it before. I've studied it over and over again because it was a photo that almost broke my heart. It's Duncan, and a pretty girl with her arm wrapped around his waist as she reaches up on her tiptoes to kiss him.

'It's you?' I say. 'You're Dr B. You're the one who sent me the photo of Duncan. Who wanted to make me think he was cheating on me? You're the one who's been doing all of this to me? Making me think I'm going insane?'

'He's not good enough for you, Frankie. I don't know why you can't see it. You need someone stable. Someone with a good job and a steady income who's not out half the time. I wish you could see you deserve more than that.'

I have a horrible feeling I know exactly where this is going.

'Like you, you mean?'

But rather than answering the way I expect him to, he looks almost disgusted by the suggestion.

'I just want to keep you safe, Frankie.'

An iciness prickles across the back of my neck.

'What is this, Will? Why are you doing this to me?'

'Maybe it's easier if you see for yourself.'

He gestures to the walls and the other photos.

I inch towards them. A couple of them contain what look like a young Will with a woman who I assume is his mother. They have the same brassy blonde hair, the same narrow eyes. I scan across them, searching for some sign of familiarity, when I look at the next one. This one is clearly a full family photograph. Young Will is there, centre again, although he's older than in the original photo. He's sitting on a moped with an L plate on the front. If I had to guess, I'd say it's a birthday gift, judging from the bow on the front, but my eyes don't linger on the bike or Will. Instead, they shift to the two adults standing behind him with their arms looped over one another's shoulders. The woman is the same one as in the other photos, the one with the brassy hair, but it's the man who makes me feel nauseous. The way he's staring at the camera, it's like he's looking straight at me. Like he knows exactly who it is he's staring at. All the air has been drained from the room and from my lungs, which is why when I finally manage to speak, my voice comes out as a croak.

'Why the fuck do you have photos of my father?'

73

There's no mistaking it. If I hadn't been 100 per cent certain looking at the photo with the bike, then the other dozen of him make me absolutely sure that these are photos of my father. There's one of him in the early noughties, sporting the same dated moustache he had in all my baby photos. And he's holding a baby in some of these too, only it's not me. This one has far lighter hair and is wrapped in a yellow teddy-bear suit. It looks nothing like me.

'Did you photoshop these?' I say. 'What the hell is this? What are you doing? Is this to do with the ghost-writing? If this is your idea of research, you took it too far. Way, way too far. Oh my God, you were the one who was following me, weren't you? It was you? You were stalking me.'

He grimaces. 'I think of it as protecting, Frankie. Everything I've ever done is to help you. Right from the beginning, from Gloria to—'

'Gloria?' I cut across him. 'What do you know about Gloria?'

'I've been there from the beginning, Frankie. I was the one who told her to go to you. To help you. I would have gone myself, but I suspected you'd be far more suspicious of a young man wanting a room in a house where a double murder took place than a scatty girl like her. She was my way of watching you. To help. I was there at the beginning and, yes, I was there at the end too.'

I can't digest everything he's saying. I know I need to, but there's too much to take in. Question after question forms in my mouth and I can't get them out quick enough.

'It was you, wasn't it? You were the one who rang Duncan. Who told him she'd died?'

'I know. I know, I'm sorry to do it that way, but I hoped that perhaps, if you seemed a little unstable, it might give Duncan the final push he needed to leave you. You were never going to find someone good enough while he was on the scene.'

'A little unstable? You made me look fucking crazy!'

I turn in a circle, my fingers digging into my scalp. When I finally stop moving, I look straight at him.

'Where is she?' I say. 'What did you do to her?'

For the first time, he looks at me with a sense of pity. Worry, even.

'She was going to tell you, Frankie. She was going to tell you I'd paid her to move into your house. To help you. And then to leave.'

'You did what?'

'It was for the best. She didn't want to leave. I think it's only fair I tell you that. She actually thought your friendship was real, but you needed to move on with your life. She wasn't a stable person, Frankie. She did drugs, you know. Before I found her to help us. To help you. And she went that way again. It was best for her in the long run. She's at peace now.'

'No... no.' My hands cover my mouth and the sounds of my

breath echo into my ears. 'When? When did she die? I checked the hospitals. But the internet… the computer…'

'Ahh.' His eyes widen, like I've actually said something to surprise him. 'You checked obituaries online? Smart. But obviously, you didn't check very closely. If you had, then you'd have seen that the Gloria Noland who died six months ago was eighty-nine.'

'What?'

'Yes. Our Gloria's grandmother. On her maternal side. I will admit, I gave her a helping hand too, but that was purely out of kindness. I hate to see a person suffer. And it may have helped to keep our Gloria in line.'

He's insane. There is no doubt. But he's still not making sense.

'You're saying I did speak to Gloria then? But she's dead now? But the hospitals. I rang the hospitals.'

'You're not keeping up, Frankie,' he says, lifting his hands into the air. 'Come on. I thought you were smarter than that. Gloria was the name we decided she should use. A homage to Grandmother, but also we thought it might bring you a little hope. A little light. And it did for a while, didn't it? But had she come back into your life, she would have ruined things. She would have been a bad influence on you. Just like that Heidi person. You needed her out of your life too.'

I don't want to listen. I don't want to hear any more, but every time he speaks, it's like another piece of the jigsaw puzzle has slotted into place.

'You told the university about the affair?'

'To be fair, I warned him first. I did. I thought the blackmail would be enough. Yet he persisted.'

'What the fuck? You were blackmailing Dr Jarvis?'

'To introduce you into his ghost-writing team, yes. So I could help you. Help you with money. Help you with your writing. Help you tap into that part of yourself you don't want to admit is there. But it is. I know it is, Frankie, because I have that part in me too.'

I can't take it all in. I don't even know how I'm still standing. Maybe because I know that if I collapse, it's going to make it a damn sight harder to get out of here.

'You were going to kill Heidi too,' I say. 'The influencer. The carbon monoxide. Did you poison her? Have you already done it? Oh God, please say she's safe.'

He lets out a slight laugh.

'It was on my list to do, if she continued to abuse your friendship, but thankfully your relationship seems to have found a natural end, so we'll see.'

A natural end? There was nothing natural about it. He was the one who turned her against me. Trying to block out everything else, I focus on the here and now. Once again, my eyes fall on the photos. 'Why have you done this to them? What is wrong with you? Is it to make you feel like you know me or something? Because you don't. You don't know me at all, and I have no fucking idea who you are.'

'I've not done anything to these photos. These are exactly as the moments happened. Exactly as the memories are etched in my mind. Even these.' He steps forward and lightly touches the ones where my father is holding a baby that is not me. 'I might not remember it clearly, but it has an effect, doesn't it? All those early moments, they form our conscious memories. The parts of us that shape who we are to become. That's what's happening here. He was building me. Creating the person I came to be.'

'You're insane.'

I don't care about staying calm any more. I can't stay calm. Will is crazy. I don't even know if half of what he's telling me is the truth or pure delusion, and I don't care. I just want to get as far away from him as possible.

'You need to let me out of here, because if you don't, I will hurt you. I promise that.'

'You won't do that,' he says calmly. 'You need to know the truth, just like I needed the truth. We're so similar. Of course we are. That's the way it's meant to be, isn't it?'

I edge away, trying to stay as steady as I can. I want to run. More than anything, I want to turn around and run away from here as fast as I can, but I heard that lock click in the door when he closed it. He would be on me before I could get out. All I can do is keep talking until I work out what it is he wants and hopefully negotiate my way out of here.

'Why would you say that?' I ask, keeping my eyes on him but edging back towards the door. 'Why would you think we're similar? Because we both do English? Because we both write novels? Really?'

His face crinkles, but beneath the look of confusion, there seems to be something else there too. Hurt. But why would he be hurt?

'No, of course I don't think that's why we're the same. But it makes sense that we should both be drawn towards the same things, doesn't it? After all, lots of siblings are.'

'Siblings?' I shake my head.

'Why don't you understand, Frankie? Why don't you see what I'm trying to tell you? Why I've needed to help you all this time. I'm your brother.'

74

This has to be the sickest joke anyone has ever tried to pull. This man – the lecturer's assistant, who I've had less than a dozen conversations with – has locked me in his bedroom and is telling me I'm his sister? It doesn't make sense.

'I don't have any siblings,' I say with a firmness to my tone. 'I'm an only child.'

'I know that's what you believe. You believed you were an only child with a doting mother and a father who was gone half of the year. A father who was always taking trips away because he worked as a long-distance lorry driver. That's what he told us, at least. And I know from Gloria he told you the same. That's something, isn't it? That he kept his lies consistent with us both.'

There's no moisture left in my mouth or throat, and yet I try swallowing repeatedly. All it's doing is creating a larger lump that refuses to go down.

'You didn't know my father.'

'Yes. Yes, I did. Your father was a liar. Like mine was a liar. He was a gambler. A waster. He could barely hold down a job for six months, but it never mattered because his family didn't see enough of him to know. Don't you think it's funny that when your mum was killed, there was barely penny to your name? You were left with almost nothing at all. Don't you think it's strange? But there was debt, wasn't there? Debt and destruction. That's what your father left. I get it. Believe me, I do. That's why I've tried to help you. I've only ever tried to help you.'

He shifts towards me, but I put my hand out. I can feel the tremors travelling through my legs, making it harder and harder for me to stand.

'You don't have a clue what I went through.'

'Of course I do, Francesca. We are the same. These photos aren't fakes. They're not photoshopped. They're of me and my father. The man I loved and doted upon more than anyone in the world. The one who made me feel like I was his everything. But I wasn't, was I? I wasn't. Neither was my mother. And neither were you.'

His face transforms into anger. Sharp and hard, it contorts his features, and in that second, I see something. A flash. An image. He has the same shaped face as my father, that's what I think. The same shaped nose too. And ears that are a little too big for his face, just the same way mine are. I try to quash the thoughts. I won't give in to them. He's a madman. That's all this is.

'If you were so keen to help me, then how come I was nearly kicked off my course just now?'

His eyes bug from his face.

'The poem?'

I let out a sound that's remarkably close to a snarl. 'So that was you? That doesn't sound like the actions of someone who's trying to help.'

He shakes his head, and it looks, for the first time, as if I've unsteadied him.

'You were struggling. I thought... I just wanted to help you. It was mine. I wrote it. Years ago. I didn't think she'd remember. I just wanted to help you. That's all I've wanted to do, Frankie. From the moment it happened. From the moment I learned about you. I promised that. I promised, and I keep my promises.'

'Who did you promise? What are you talking about?'

He's the one clutching at his head now. Pushing his fingers into the back of his skull like he's trying to block out his thoughts.

Yet there's something else still niggling in the back of my mind. Something that won't quite fit, like trying to turn the wrong key before it's all the way into the lock. I'm trying to make it make sense when the words he used while talking about Gloria suddenly fall into place.

'You said it was a double murder. Double murder. You didn't say murder-suicide. Everyone says murder-suicide. No one believed me when I said it was a double murder. But you said double murder. Those were the words you said. Double murder.'

I know how many times I've repeated the words, but I need to. I need to know I'm not going insane.

A slight smile forms on Will's lips as tears glaze his eyes.

'You're so smart, Frankie. So smart, I was almost jealous when I read that story of yours. The rawness. The purity. I even wondered if it had been necessary to blackmail Professor Jarvis into signing you up, but I wanted to make sure. I wanted to make sure I could help you the way you needed to be helped.'

He's avoiding it. Avoiding saying the words I need to hear from him. But I need to hear his answer. I have to. So with my heart lodged so far up my throat I'm barely able to breathe, I choke out the words.

'You did it, didn't you?' I say. 'You killed my parents. You killed them both.'

75

I never thought I would get the chance to look my parents' murderer in the eye. That I would learn what I always believed in the bottom of my heart was true and that my father wasn't responsible. And yet now I know I was right all along.

'Did you kill them? Did you kill my mother and father?' I say, looking Will square in the eye. The fear has gone now. I don't care about myself or if he kills me. It doesn't matter. I just need to know the truth. I need to hear it come from his lips.

Will's jaw twitches, like a visible representation of the words that he's chewing over and over in his mind.

'I've been looking after you, Frankie. I've been doing a good job. The job teaching English online when you ran out of money? That was because of me. I was the one who told Gloria to make you go for that job. I interviewed you. You didn't know it, but that was the first time. The first time we spoke. And I made her make you go to those grief sessions. And the scholarship to the university. I was the one who gave Gloria all the information to pass onto you. And I rewrote your submission when it came into the department so that I knew you'd get it. I've been looking after you, Frankie.'

'My parents,' I say, my gaze unblinking. 'I won't listen to another word you say unless you tell me about them.'

His Adam's apple jerks in his throat before he offers the swiftest nod.

'He was a liar, Frankie. I didn't want to believe it, but he was. I knew what he was the day I found another phone in his coat pocket. He said it was someone else's, but there was a photo of you and that other woman on the lock screen and somehow, I knew.'

'That other woman?' I go to lunge for him, only to pull myself up just before I do. I'm furious, but I'm not stupid. 'Her name was Marian. She was my mother.' I take another pause before I carry on. 'So you found out about us, and you killed them both. That's what happened, right? You killed them both, and now what, you want to kill me, the last piece of evidence?'

'What? No. I didn't come to kill you. I just want to know you. That's all. I've spent so long staying away from you, trying to be… But we need each other now. We're all we have left.'

'I'm not anything to you. We don't have anything in common. You're a murderer, for fuck's sake. A serial killer.'

His eyes flash. 'Rupert Fitzherbert was a disgusting man. He was vile. Although I was too infatuated with him to see it at first. He knew I was his student, but he didn't care. He was blinded by his own greed and self-importance. To give him his dues, he taught me a lot about poker in those brief months together, and then he was done with me. Tossed me aside like I was nothing.'

'You killed him because he dumped you?' I say, unable to hide the disbelief in my voice.

'No, I got him fired because of that. I killed him because of the way he spoke to you – I saw it. I listened to him spew that vitriol at you, my sister—'

'I'm not your sister,' I say, but he carries on like he didn't hear me.

'I heard what he said, and I knew he couldn't stay alive. It was time anyone else was spared his malevolence.'

I don't want to hear anything more, but the door is locked and there's no way for me to get out without getting those keys off him. He's not calm enough to give them to me and let me go, which means I need to think of another plan. One that leaves him incapacitated. But it's going to take time to work that out, to think things through carefully. There's no point just picking up the bedside lamp and hoping I can get a good swing across his skull with it. Not when it's plugged into the wall. I need to be smarter than that. Which is why I ask the one question I want to hear the answer to less than any other in the entire world.

'Tell me,' I say, looking him straight in the eye as I speak. 'Tell me how my parents died.'

76

The moment I pose the question, I see the shift. The relief. This whole situation has been building up to now. A chance for him to unburden himself. Perhaps to even ask for my forgiveness, though that's sure as hell never going to happen.

Part of me wants to sit down, either on the edge of his bed or on his desk chair, but then it'll be far harder to run away if I'm seated. Still, as I look at the chair, another thought strikes. It's heavy. It could work. I move myself towards it, as if I'm preparing to take a seat, only to rest my hands on the top instead. I shift it a little, judging the weight. It's heavy, but not so heavy that I can't swing it. Perfect.

'I need to know what happened. I need to know – why did you kill her? Why did you kill my mother?'

There is no flash of guilt on his face, no expression of remorse. His face remains completely impassive, even as he perches himself on the edge of his desk.

'I didn't go there to do it. You need to believe me. I wanted to speak to her, that was all. I wanted her to know the truth. After I found his phone, the pictures of you and her on the screen, I confronted him. Obviously, he lied. That's all he ever did. He said it was a work friend's phone. One that was left in a lorry and he was going to give it back the next time he saw them. And I believed him. Only three weeks later, he was back from work again and I found the same phone, this time hidden in the garage. It was in a drawer at the bottom of the gun cabinet.'

'Why did he even have a gun?' I say, voicing a question that's been playing on my mind for over half a decade. 'He was always against shooting?'

'Maybe with you, with your family. But it was different with us. He was different. Maybe that's how he excused what he was doing. He could be different parts of himself with my mother and with yours. Different people entirely, almost. He couldn't have guns and shoot animals with your mum, but mine... She'd grown up like that. It offered him the sense of freedom that he needed.'

I want to snap back at him, to say that my mother offered him all the freedom he could ever have wanted, that they were in love and there was nothing lacking in their relationship, but I don't. I don't want to draw attention to myself and nor do I want to stop his narrative. Not when I'm so close to learning a truth I've needed for over a quarter of my life.

'So you found the phone?' I say, prompting him to continue.

Will nods. 'This time, I was certain he was lying, and I was going to get proof. I just needed to work out his password to get in. That was my plan, though it wasn't as easy as I'd hoped. Do you know how many four-digit combinations you can make for a passcode? Ten thousand. Ten thousand. He was home for two weeks, and I still didn't manage to get in, so I knew I needed a different option. So I followed him.'

'You could drive?' I say. 'You could drive to follow him?'

I don't know why I make such a comment. Maybe because I had only just passed my test when my parents died and I couldn't have dreamt of successfully trailing someone. I still don't think I could. While I don't know how old Will is, my best guess is that he's the same age as me, give or take a few months.

'Of course I could drive. I was twenty-one,' he replies.

'Twenty-one?' I frown. 'You were twenty-one when they died?'

He pauses and tilts his head to the side a little as he speaks. 'You don't get it, do you?'

'Get what?'

'I'm older than you. Our dad... he was with our family first. You're the other family. The bastard child. The one who shouldn't be here. You. Not me.'

77

It's too much. It's all too much. Finding out my father had another family on the side, that he cheated on my mother and brought up another child without us ever knowing about it, is horrific. But this… We are the other family. We are the dirty secret. But how? How did none of this come out after his death?

'I suspect that was the reason he never married either of our mothers,' Will says, breaking the silence as he reads my thoughts. 'Paperwork makes it harder to keep lies going, I guess.'

It's too much to get my head around. I am the one that needed to be kept hidden. That was probably why we had to keep moving so often. I want to pass out. How the hell did he do it? How the hell did he get away with it for so long?

'So, you followed him,' I say. I need to get back to Will's story, mainly to stop myself from overthinking. If I lose myself in my thoughts, then there's no way I'll get out of here alive.

'I did,' Will says. 'He drove for seven hours, with stops, that is. Once, I thought I was going to run out of petrol, and the whole thing would be a bust. Another time, I was sure he had spotted me following him. After all, he was the one who'd bought me the car. I felt certain he'd recognise it following him off every roundabout and through every junction. Sometimes I think he was just too self-absorbed to think he could ever get caught, but other times... I don't know, other times I wonder if he actually knew. If he actually wanted me to follow him, to find out the truth.'

A silence settles between us. One in which I'm sure Will's mind is retracing that day. Seven hours of anticipation, that ended up in death. Was he planning their murder the entire journey?

'So what happened? You reached our house, saw my mum, and shot her?'

He shakes his head. 'That's not how it happened. I swear, I didn't go there to kill her.'

'But you brought the gun with you? People don't bring guns unless they're planning on using them.'

He continues to shake his head. Despite the fact that only five minutes ago, he near enough admitted to killing a lecturer because they dumped him, he's obviously upset by my accusation.

'It felt like the right thing. For safety, I think. I didn't know where I was going. I can't explain it. But I swear on your life, Frankie, I hadn't planned on killing her.'

His eyes stare up at me, and I have no choice but to nod. To act as though I believe him. Whether I do or not, I haven't decided. What I do know is that I don't trust him as far as I can throw him.

'So then what? You followed him to the house?'

'I didn't. I went into the house to see. The back door was open, and they were there, in the living room, laughing together. Catching up. And I had the gun. I don't know why I'd brought it; I promise you, it had never been my intention to hurt her. I wanted her to know the truth. For him to own up to what he did. That was all. But when I saw them together, when I saw how at ease he was, how he was lying to her without blinking an eye, I couldn't help it. I knew then I was going to shoot.'

I can see the image in my mind, playing like a video recording. I see my father and the way he would always lean forward so that his hands rested on my mum's knees, and she would automatically drop her head onto his shoulder. And Will, young and heartbroken, discovering the man he viewed as a hero had been lying to him for his entire life.

'I told her to get out,' Will says. His voice cracks as he speaks. 'I didn't want to hurt her. I told her to get out. But she wouldn't. She wouldn't leave him. It didn't matter what I said to her. She wouldn't go. "He's my father," I told her again and again, but she didn't listen. And... he just stood there, weeping in disbelief. He didn't even say my name. He just began to cry. And she... well, she tried to get the gun off me. I swear, Frankie, I swear it was an accident. I didn't want to kill her. I didn't. I hadn't come there to do that. But when the gun went off...' He stops. Tears are rolling down his cheeks as he tries to sniff them away. As much as I don't want to, I can see it's the truth. He's telling the truth.

'And so what about Dad?' I say, still having to force myself to breathe. I wish I could stop the tears from escaping, but I can't. I can't stop them any more than Will can, and I hate that similarity between us. 'Was his death an accident, too?'

Will sniffs again, this time wiping his face with the back of his hand before he straightens up and looks directly at me.

'No,' he says. 'No. But it wasn't like I had a choice. I promise you, Frankie. I didn't have a choice.'

78

Tears stream now, stopping only to pool on the top of my lip and chin before they fall to the ground. Strangely, though, there's a peace to the pain. Mum had died not knowing the truth about my father. She probably thought Will was crazy and would have assumed her death was nothing more than a tragic accident at the hand of a madman. I'm grateful for that. Grateful that she didn't learn about the betrayal she had suffered. That she was the other woman. The dirty secret. Still, I need the rest of the story. I need to know about Dad, about how he died.

'You shot him then?' I ask. 'That was it. My mother was lying there dying, and you shot him too. Made it look like a suicide?'

'No.' Will shakes his head. 'That wasn't how it happened. I told you that.' He wipes away his tears too, but no more fall to replace them. I can already tell that the pain and grief that came with recalling my mother's death won't be there in the second half of his tale. Instead, he walks in a small circle before he stops directly in front of the chair. The chair that I still have my hands grasped firmly on the top of. This could be the moment to pick it up and swing it. To knock him down and make my escape. But there's still more I need to know.

'So, what happened?' I say. 'Will, what happened next? I need you to tell me, okay? You understand I need to know?'

I feel physically sick. Using that soft tone with him causes the bile to rise at the back of my throat, but I have to fight it down. If the only way for me to get out of here is by leaving Will with no pulse, then I'll do it, but I want to make sure I know the whole story beforehand. I'm done with half-truths.

'I wanted to call an ambulance.' Will's eyes are unblinking as he stares at me. 'I promise on your life. I said we should probably call an ambulance, but he was crying. Crying at her, but then he was yelling. Yelling at me? For an accident?'

There's such disbelief in Will's voice, it sounds almost naïve. He's insane, I can see that, but how insane? Insane enough that he would have made this entire story up? That he's merely a stalker with an elaborate imagination? It could be possible. He could have just photoshopped the images. But as I look at him there, his sandy blonde hair the same colour as mine, his stance, weighted on his left side like I do, I believe him. I do. But that's good because I also know that if what he really wants is our friendship, then I have a way out of this situation, and I am going to use it.

'The things he was saying to me.' He shudders as if the memory has a physical hold on him. 'Fathers shouldn't speak that way to their sons. They shouldn't. He should have known it was an accident. He should have believed me.'

'And that made you kill him?'

He shakes his head. 'He was blaming me, but he was the reason I was there. He tried to place it all on me, and I wasn't having it. It wasn't my fault. You get that, right? It wasn't my fault. He was to blame. Their deaths weren't my fault. They were his.'

He sounds so young, like a child seeking his parent's absolution for a mistake he's made, or worse still, his sibling's.

'Right,' I say, but something about his words catches in my ear. The plural. *Their* deaths.

'You mean Rupert, right? Is that who you mean? Are you saying my father is somehow to blame for what you did to Rupert? That it was because of all the hurt he caused you?'

At this, Will scrunches up his nose as he looks at me.

'No, I mean theirs. My mother and yours. He has to take the blame for both of them. Both of their deaths.'

79

It's like every time I get my head around the story, he adds another piece that makes it impossible for me to follow. Three deaths. That's more than enough blood for anyone to have on their hands. But he killed his mother too? Any hope that being his sibling – or at least him thinking I am – was going to save me is rapidly evaporating.

'Your mum? You hurt your mum too?'

A look of disgust forms on his face. 'No, no, I'd never hurt her. Never!' For a split second, I think he's going to strike me, and I tighten my grasp on the chair, but then pain shrouds his expression as he shakes his head. 'I should have thought, though,' he says. 'I should have realised. She was too gentle. She couldn't cope with it. I should have known that.'

'Tell me,' I say. 'I won't judge you. I promise.'

And then, for the first time, I do something that sickens me to my core – I step towards him and rest one hand on his shoulder. A tiny gesture, and it's the most I can manage, but as he looks up at me, his face gleams, like that single touch has made it all worthwhile.

'You wouldn't leave me, would you?' He sniffles as he speaks. 'You understand, don't you?'

'I do. You can tell me, Will. You can tell me what happened to your mum.'

He nods, freeing a stray tear which trickles downwards towards his jaw.

'I thought it was the right thing to do,' he says, sniffing as he struggles to get his words out. 'I made him call her and tell her that things were over. Tell her that he'd been seeing someone else. I made him put her on speakerphone too, just so I knew he wasn't lying and he was really telling her.'

'You called your mother while mine was dying in her home?'

I don't hide the repulsion in my voice, yet he doesn't seem to hear. He's lost in the darkness of his memories. 'Her voice... I should have known. But he told her what he'd done. He said I was fucking insane. Said I'd killed someone. She thought he was lying, but I told her. I told her who it was. What he'd done. If I'd left, then... It was a mistake. I didn't realise what she'd do. If I'd left then, maybe I'd have been able to stop her. But the drive was long, right? I told you that, didn't I? It was seven hours long. She took some pills. By the time I got there, she was already cold.'

My hands are trembling. Anger, disbelief, disgust or fear? I don't know which emotion is causing the effect, but it doesn't matter. One way or another, I'm running out of time. I can feel that.

'So you just watched my mother die?'

'Even when I hung up the phone, Dad was still insisting that we had to call an ambulance, but I could see it was too late. I think he could too. He kept saying that you'd come home soon, that you'd come home and you couldn't see this. It wasn't fair. He kept saying that. It wasn't fair on you. Like it was fair on me. So I lifted the gun up to his temples. He didn't stop speaking, though.

I remember that. I remember how he didn't stop speaking. He kept talking about you. Making me promise that I wouldn't let you find out. That I wouldn't let it ruin your life. "She's your little sister." That's what he kept saying to me. "Big brothers are supposed to look after their little sisters." But I have been, haven't I? I've been doing it, right? I've been protecting you. Looking after you. I've been a good big brother, haven't I, Frankie?'

As he looks me in the eye, his question hanging in the air between us, I pick up the chair that's in my grip and swing it with all the strength I can muster, straight into the side of his skull.

80

Moments shape our lives. Sometimes, they are small moments, instances during which we fail to realise the significance until long after the time has passed. That failed grade on a test that made us rethink our career trajectory. The house move we took, not knowing that friendship, and perhaps more, was waiting around the corner.

Others are bigger incidents. Getting a promotion which means taking a job abroad, losing a loved one, or finding one. But what if the incidents that have shaped our lives – my life as an only child, my murderous father, my friend who helped me rebuild myself after my loss – are all lies? These incidents were paramount in me becoming who I've become, and yet they were falsehoods that were fed to me knowingly and willingly by people I trusted. But this moment, what happens between me and Will in this room, is going to shape what type of life I have, or even if I have a life at all, from this point on. And I'm sure as hell not letting anyone else have any control over it this time.

Blood is seeping from his skull out onto the carpet, spreading towards me. I bend downwards, trying to steady my breathing, but the cloying, metallic scent grows thicker and thicker in my lungs with every inhale. With my eyes scrunched and half closed, I feel down Will's legs, patting down his pockets and searching for the keys. It takes less than half a minute for me to find them, and with a whimper of relief, I slip my hand inside the fabric. My fingertips have just touched the cold metal of the keys when he grasps my forearm.

'You can't... You won't...' His voice is a gurgling wheeze and his pupils are so dilated, there is no colour to his irises any more. 'Frankie?'

'I'm sorry. Really, I'm sorry, Will.'

I grab his hand, shake him off, pull out the key, and don't look back.

It takes several attempts to unlock the door, probably because of how my hand is shaking, but the moment it springs open, I start to run.

Even when I'm outside, I don't slow down. I take the stairs in near leaps before I run out onto the street. I can still smell the blood. He looked like he couldn't stand, but what if it was an act? What if any second now, he's going to sprint out of his apartment and want recompense for what I just did?

I've got my bag. It's still on my back the same way it was when we walked here, with my phone in the pocket. I need to ring the police. And an ambulance. But to do that I need to stop, unzip my bag, and use my phone, and I don't want to stop running until I'm surrounded by people. I need to be somewhere where I'm safe. My feet pound against the ground, while my lungs wheeze from tears and lack of exercise. I can't stop, though. He might be behind me. I need to get away. As far away as possible.

I reach a main road, with two coffee shops on the opposite corners of a junction. Finally, I slow my pace. There are people here. Lots of people, and several of them are looking at me. It's only when I reach for my phone that I realise why. There's blood all up my top. It must have got there from when I reached down to get the keys from Will's pocket.

For a second, I stare at it. So much blood. The way it's spread up the fabric. The way it was spreading across the carpet. Can someone survive that much blood loss? Do I want them to?

'Frankie?'

My head snaps up.

'Oh my God, Frankie? What happened? Are you hurt? Oh God, we need to call an ambulance.'

'Duncan?' His hands are on me, but I flinch away. 'How did you find me? How did you...'

He lifts up his phone and I think I'm going to see the numbers 999 there on the screen, but instead, I see a map. A map with a small blue dot flashing on it.

'I don't understand?' I say. I deleted the app from his phone. I'm sure I did.

'We put the location apps on our computers too. Remember? In case they were ever nicked, so that we could find them. I reloaded it on my phone from there. What the hell's happened?'

'Well I'm not crazy. That's the first thing.'

EPILOGUE

Calling the police wasn't exactly straightforward as I didn't know the address I'd been to. Duncan had the street name; that was where he was going to before I began running, but I had to meet the police outside and direct them to the correct house. They cordoned off the area and waited for the ambulance to arrive. The body bag told me what I already suspected. Will was dead.

The entire time, Duncan didn't let go of my hand. When the police said they would need to question me on my own, he kicked up such a fuss, I thought he was going to get himself arrested, but for once, I knew the right thing to say.

'I can do this, Duncan,' I said. 'It's okay, I'll talk to them, and then we'll go home. Together. Please.'

'I'm so sorry, Frankie. I should have believed you.'

'Really? I'm not sure I would have if it was the other way around.'

It took a basic DNA test to confirm that, yes, Will and I were half-siblings. The images of me, and the emails from Dr B were enough to convince the police that I was correct about the stalking. That I had been held against my will, and my act of killing my own flesh and blood had been self-defence.

Still, it was months until all the proceedings were wrapped up. Fortunately, I'd had plenty of things to keep me distracted.

'I can't believe you had three agents battling for you,' Heidi says as we sit sipping our coffees together. 'Well, actually, I can. The book is going to be such a hit; I can feel it.'

'I'm just glad I've got it written,' I say honestly. 'It was fairly tough-going at times.' Writing a thriller about a girl stalked by a brother she didn't know existed didn't require that much on the research front, and though the process was mostly cathartic, it also meant facing things about my past that I'd have rather blocked out.

'Well, Ivor and I will want several signed copies. We're already starting a library for this one, not that they'll be able to read your book for a long while, obviously.' As she finishes talking, she offers her growing bump a rub. Professor Jarvis had returned to work after his shotgun marriage to Heidi. He'd assured the faculty that he had proposed long before the relationship was discovered, but due to his history with relationships, he had wanted to keep it a secret. The university clearly didn't want any more drama, and so they were happy to accept this blatant lie.

'Any more thoughts about what you're going to do with the money from the ghost-writing?' Heidi asks when she stops rubbing her belly. 'I'm so glad they gave it all to you. I can't believe you haven't spent it already, though. I would have taken it all and gone on some massive holiday. Although people pay me to go on holiday and review their hotels, so I probably wouldn't need to.'

I let out a slight chuckle. The fact that Heidi is just the same, after everything we've been through, is always a comfort.

Given that Will had already paid for the ghost-writing project in full, all involved agreed that the remaining £45,000 should go to me, and I was not expected to write another word for it. To be honest, though, it'll probably be paying for therapy for the rest of my life, but that's okay.

'I'm not sure,' I reply. 'We might put it towards a house deposit, but I didn't want to spend any until the inquest was over. Speaking of which, I need to go to the police station. Will's belongings have finally been released. They've said I can go collect them.'

'Do you want them?' she says, a look of near repulsion on her face.

It's a good question and not one I have an answer to yet.

'I'm going to collect them regardless. I mean, I might end up burning it all, but I think I'll just see how I feel. It's photos mainly. There might be one or two of my dad that I want to keep.'

'Well, if you want me to come over and look through anything with you, you know I'm always here.'

'Thank you. I do.'

Three hours later, I'm on the bus with a large envelope in my arms, heading back home, and I already know curiosity is going to get the better of me. I want to look at them at least once, even if I *am* just going to burn them afterwards, and there's no time like the present.

The moment I'm home, I tip them out onto the floor.

There's no rhyme or reason to how they're arranged. Each photo I pick up shows the subjects at a completely different stage of their life, though I try to use a combination of Will's age and Dad's facial hair to estimate how long ago they were taken. I try not to look at ones of his mother too much. Somehow, the knowledge of her pain resonates through the image more fiercely than with Will or Dad. Probably because I know that like us, she was a real victim in all this.

Despite trying to avoid looking at her, the last photo I pick up is one of her and Dad. By the looks of it, they're in the hospital, holding Will as a baby. There's a smile on her face. But it's shallow, and the exhaustion has aged her. She looks about ten years older than in lots of the other photos. I guess labour does that to a person. I'm not sure if I'll find that out. Duncan and I have set a date for a wedding – town hall, reception with his band at the pub – but we're non-committal on children for now, and that's fine.

I'm about to put all the photos back when I see another one stuck in the envelope. With a slight tug, I release it. It's almost identical to the one I was just looking at. My dad is still beaming and Will's mum has the same tired look on her face and the baby in her arms, but this one is panned slightly further out. I squint, trying to make sense of what I'm seeing. A young boy, about ten years old, is grinning madly at the baby. Not just any young boy, though. One I recognise from all the other photos. It's Will. It's a photo of Will with his parents in a hospital. My heart hitches in my chest. If Will is in the photo, then who the hell is this baby?

I look at the photo once more, then close my eyes and draw in a long breath. Paranoia is understandable after what I've been through. That's what my therapist says. And that's all this is. Paranoia. Nothing more. I open my eyes again and slip the photo back into the envelope. I'm done focusing on the past. I've got a future to start building.

* * *

MORE FROM H.M. LYNN

Another book from H.M. Lynn, *The Head Teacher*, is available to order now here:

https://mybook.to/TheHeadTeacherBackAd

ABOUT THE AUTHOR

H. M. Lynn writes tense, gripping psychological thrillers with her signature engaging and emotionally rich storytelling. She also writes in many other genres including romance, as Hannah Lynn.

Sign up to H. M. Lynn's mailing list for news, competitions and updates on future books.

Visit H. M. Lynn's website: www.hannahlynnauthor.com

Follow H. M. Lynn on social media:

- facebook.com/hannahlynnauthor
- instagram.com/hannahlynnwrites
- tiktok.com/@hannah.lynn.romcoms
- bookbub.com/authors/hannah-lynn

THE Murder LIST

THE MURDER LIST IS A NEWSLETTER DEDICATED TO SPINE-CHILLING FICTION AND GRIPPING PAGE-TURNERS!

SIGN UP TO MAKE SURE YOU'RE ON OUR HIT LIST FOR EXCLUSIVE DEALS, AUTHOR CONTENT, AND COMPETITIONS.

SIGN UP TO OUR NEWSLETTER

BIT.LY/THEMURDERLISTNEWS

Boldwood

Boldwood Books is an award-winning fiction publishing company seeking out the best stories from around the world.

Find out more at www.boldwoodbooks.com

Join our reader community for brilliant books, competitions and offers!

Follow us
@BoldwoodBooks
@TheBoldBookClub

Sign up to our weekly deals newsletter

https://bit.ly/BoldwoodBNewsletter

Printed in Great Britain
by Amazon